Into the Shimmering Light

Stories

Into the Shimmering Light

Stories

Rich Thayer

Old Vine Books LLC

In memory of my parents,
Richard E. and Ann D. Thayer

Special thanks to my wife, Glenda, and
our adult children, Janet and Rick,
for their support, encouragement,
and input to these stories.

"You look for a light, a light that shimmers to attract you.
You'll know it when you see it, but you have to search for
it. When you see it, pursue it to wherever it takes you."

— An old time friend

Contents

Why Polar Bears Swim

MILL RAPIDS, Ohio — Jan. 1, 1972 — Every New Years Day, Emery Adams walked across River Road, past the elementary school, and to the bank of the river. He removed his coat, shoes, socks, shirt, and pants, then, wearing only a bathing suit, walked through the snow to the water's edge. Some years, he'd carry an axe to chop away any ice that had accumulated in the calm waters near shore. Then he would step into the 40-degree water. Then another step. And another. Across the limestone riverbed until he reached the deeper water where he would fall forward, allowing the churning current to engulf his body.

Lenny, Charlie, and I were high school freshmen, and this was our first time witnessing this event. We were among a dozen spectators that year. Back then, not many people knew about this. It was publicized only by word of mouth in those days. They said this was the 36th time Emery took his New Year's Day plunge. They said he started this tradition as a way to celebrate his wedding anniversary. Most of his swims were without spectators, but now at age 65, he was beginning to attract a small audience.

Charlie is the one that heard about it and invited us to come. He said there'd be some other kids from school here, and he was right. As we stood on the snowy riverbank, I could tell which of those other kids he really wanted to see. Charlie's eyes were not on Emery, paddling like a polar bear in the rushing water. Charlie's eyes were on Jackie.

I didn't blame him. Jackie was a cool girl, a freshman cheerleader who looked great in a short cheerleading skirt. She was energetic and sassy. She always had a pretty smile when I passed her between classes at school. The problem for Charlie, though, was that her boyfriend always had his arm around her waist, and he was a senior. Of course, that didn't stop Charlie from pursuing her.

Emery came to his feet in the river and returned to shore, jogging in place as he wrapped himself in a towel. The small crowd cheered and gathered around him. Some snapped photos.

"How do you feel?" someone shouted.

"I feel great," he replied. "I'm the warmest person here."

The three of us moved in closer, and Charlie managed to position us right behind Jackie.

"Hey Doug, would you ever do that?" Charlie asked me in a voice louder than necessary.

"No way," I replied.

"How about you, Lenny?"

"Not me. If I didn't drown or freeze to death, my parents would kill me."

"You guys are chickens. I think it would be cool," Charlie said.

"You probably need a permit to swim here," Lenny speculated.

"That wouldn't stop me," Charlie boasted. "I'd be in and out before anyone could catch me."

Emery was dry, dressed, and heading home, and the crowd was beginning to disperse. Jackie turned around to face Charlie.

"Are you going to do it?" she asked.

"I might."

"Then let's see you."

"I'd do it today, but I don't have my bathing suit."

"Just take off your clothes and jump in. Everyone is leaving, you'd be in and out before anyone would see you. Or are you a chicken?" she challenged.

"Let's do it together."

"OK, you first," she countered.

Charlie studied her subtly freckled face, her sassy smile, and those green eyes that sparkled with confidence that he would wiggle out of his bravado. But she didn't know Charlie. He took her hand. "Come on," he said, and led her to the water's edge.

Charlie took off his stocking cap and gave it to Jackie. He took off his heavy coat and gave that to her. Then his sweat shirt. His T-shirt. Charlie's eyes were fixed on Jackie's eyes, and her eyes were fixed on Charlie's muscular chest. Something changed as I watched them. Jackie's sassiness ebbed. Charlie's confidence flowed.

"Oh God," Lenny said, "he's going to do it."

"Nah, he won't," I said.

Charlie reached to his belt and pulled the loose end out of the loop. He pulled it so the pin dropped out of the hole. He unbuttoned his jeans, then slowly unzipped them.

From the road, a car approached, it's horn honking. It was a 1968 Mustang fastback with the driver's window down and Jackie's boyfriend leaning out. Jackie turned to see him, dropped Charlie's clothes in the snow, and ran to the car.

Charlie smiled as he buttoned his jeans, buckled his belt, put on his T-shirt and sweatshirt, and donned his coat and hat. His face was aglow with confidence. Even though Jackie had run to her boyfriend, Charlie knew his gambit had succeeded.

We set out on our walk to our homes, and the question that followed me home was *Why?* Why would Emery take this plunge every year? He could drown. He could have a heart attack. He could get swept away by the current.

Maybe, like Charlie, he did it to get the attention of a girl, but Emery had been married for 36 years. Was this a requirement of their marriage vows? Every year, Emery must brave the icy water, and, if he lives, his wife will stick with him another year?

Or was it some kind of a religious rite? A baptism? An annual purification from the sins of the previous year?

After 36 years, wouldn't he have given up his sinful ways to obviate the need for this purification?

I had come to the river and had watched. I had applauded. Now I headed home with no idea what the event was all about. It was all risk, but what was the point? The questions persisted. *Why? Why? Why?*

MILL RAPIDS, Ohio — Jan. 1, 1978 — As I studied my way through high school, those *Why* questions were always there, not just about Emery's swim, but about everything. Why do people do the things they do? What beacon in nature draws someone into space or into a burning building or onto a concert stage? What lures someone over a waterfall in a barrel or over a row of cars on a motorcycle or into a rushing winter river? *Why?*

Along with the *Whys* were the *Whos, Whats, Whens, Wheres,* and *Hows.* They were the five W's and an H as I learned in a high school journalism class. No journalistic story was complete unless it answered them all. So my natural obsession with these questions led me to pursue journalism as a career.

I wrote for the high school newspaper and chose newspaper journalism as my course of study in college. I was now a junior in college and working part time as a reporter for the *Mill Rapids Weekly.* I wrote obituaries, engagement and wedding announcements, club news, and crime reports as well as news stories and features. In December, my editor handed me the paper's camera and asked me to cover Emery's annual swim.

It had been six years since I attended his ritual. I called Charlie and Lenny and asked them if they wanted to come with me, and we decided to meet at the Bridgewater Cafe at noon. Six years ago, it was closed on New Years Day, but thanks to the growing popularity of Emery's swim, the cafe was now open on this holiday. Emery had gained some notoriety, and that was good for business.

"How's married life?" I asked Charlie as the three of us settled in to our booth.

"Couldn't be better," he replied. "And I have big news. Jackie and I are expecting."

Lenny and I high-fived him with congratulations. Six years ago he had called Jackie's dare to swim in the cold water and had been saved only by the arrival of her boyfriend, but later that year, she left her boyfriend to go with Charlie, and they were together for the rest of high school. When they graduated, Lenny and I were among his groomsmen. Now they were starting a family.

"I'm also going to be doing interstate routes this year," he said, "between Fort Wayne and Toledo." Charlie had been driving for a trucking company since high school graduation.

"Watch out for the Mill Rapids police," I said. "I'd hate to have to include you in the crime log for speeding." The Fort Wayne to Toledo highway ran through town, and our police were crouched cats anxious to pounce on anyone exceeding the speed limit, especially truckers.

"I'm up for the challenge," he said.

I had no doubt about that. He lived for a challenge. He was energized by conflict, yet his heart was always in the right place. He was a courageous protector. He would be a good father.

"I've got some good news, too," Lenny offered. "I landed an internship."

More congratulatory high-fives. Lenny was an accounting major and, like me, a junior at the university. I could not imagine a different profession for him. He was good with numbers, but more importantly, he was particular and precise. He always followed the rules.

We finished lunch, and the waitress brought the check. Charlie and I passed it directly to Lenny and threw in some money. Lenny would have no sloppy figuring. He precisely calculated how much each of us owed including tax and a ten percent tip, and he was prepared with coinage to ensure we each paid no more or no less than what was owed. Lenny was going to make a good accountant.

We headed out of the cafe, down River Road, and past the elementary school to the river. The current was powerful that day, its waters higher than normal. The water was like a wrestler before a match, bobbing and dancing on the mat and awaiting its competitor, Emery Adams, who by then was known as the polar bear of Mill Rapids.

Spectators arrived, more than 30 by my count. They were bundled in heavy coats and scarves and trudged through the snow in their boots. I took a photo of the crowd for my article. The crowd parted as Emery arrived, then closed in a semicircle behind him, welcoming him with cheering and clapping. The 71-year-old nodded to the crowd and stripped down to his bathing suit, his mind focused on his match.

I snapped another photo, and I felt a warm sense of pride radiating from the crowd. So many had come to see him, and so many more would read about his swim in newspapers. He was a hero, a pride-worthy polar bear, a pillar of the community. His presence brought together crowds, opened restaurants on a holiday, and awoke the town during its winter hibernation.

He made his way to the water and stepped in. He bent down and tossed a chunk of ice aside, then took a few more steps until the water was up to his knees. He studied the turbulent current, sizing up his opponent, looking for the best target to attack. Then he dove forward, hands overhead, into a swirl that pulled him down and rolled him like a log.

"Knocks the breath right out of you," he yelled to the crowd as his head emerged. The crowd responded with cheers. I moved to the edge of the water, and he saw me with my camera. He looked directly at me, and I snapped another photo, then he ducked under the water again. The river was no match for him; he was as playful as a polar bear.

After a few minutes, he came out of the water, toweled off, and wrapped himself in a robe. I took another photo and stood next to him as he jogged in place.

"How do you feel?" I asked.

"I feel great. The only disagreeable thing is my fingers ache."

He said his family didn't want him to swim this year because he had recently undergone a surgery, but he dismissed their concerns. "If I'm going to have a heart attack, I might just as well have it out there," he said.

Now was the opportunity to ask my nagging question. "Why do you do it?"

He answered quickly and resolutely, "Because I'm nuts!"

The crowd laughed.

As I sat down at the typewriter that evening, I pondered his answer. It was funny, but of course it was true only in the sense that we are all nuts, and perhaps that is the honest truth. What other explanation is there for a 71-year-old man to swim in a raging, 40-degree river? What other explanation is there for 30 people to show up to watch? For restaurants to open on a holiday? For citizens to beam with pride about this hero?

I myself felt richer in my ability to say that I'm from here. I'm from the place where Emery Adams swims on New Years Day. I'd be embarrassed to do it myself. I'd fear that people would think me nuts to do such a thing, but I wouldn't hesitate to boast of being from Mill Rapids, the home of Emery Adams.

I typed my article and proofed it. Although it still had no satisfying answer to the question *Why?*, it covered well the other four W's and the H. When it was published, it would inspire pride in the community and further promote this annual event.

MILL RAPIDS, Ohio — Jan. 1, 1989 — I held one hand and Julie held the other as we walked along River Road and past the elementary school where he attended kindergarten. He was Little Doug, named after me. Julie and I met in college and married after graduation, and it wasn't long before Little Doug came along. He was five years old already, the pace of time having increased.

When we passed the elementary school, Little Doug immediately wanted to play on the playground. We promised him we'd play after, but first we needed to get to the river.

Emery was 82 years old now, but he still took his New Years Day swim. By my count, this would be his 53rd plunge. I kept count because I wanted my articles to be accurate. I worked for the *Northwest Ohio Daily* now, and I always wrote an article about this event. It was a refreshing topic to write about, a cleansing change from the usual articles about muddy electoral melees, business scandals, and crime.

Apparently, people read those articles because attendance at Emery's dip had increased steadily. As we approached the river, I counted 100 spectators awaiting Emery's arrival. We spotted Charlie and Jackie with their 10-year-old twins.

"Are you going to swim this year?" I asked Charlie.

"You know, I might — "

"You will do no such thing," Jackie interrupted. "If the twins see you do it, they will go in after you."

Julie was a little less sassy and daring now that she was a mom, but she had a good point. We were parents now, full-time examples for our children.   We had to model good behavior, safe behavior.

We were joined by Lenny and his wife.   Lenny had passed his CPA exam on his first try after college and now worked for the accounting firm at which he had interned. His wife, Doris, was an accountant for one his clients, and they quickly found reasons other than tax preparation to meet.   Charlie and I were groomsmen for him, and now they were bringing their 4-year-old daughter to see Emery swim.

Emery would have plenty of company this year because a number of Mill Rapids residents swam with him now.   So as the time approached, a parade of polar bears arrived.   Leading the parade was Emery, waving to the crowd as he hurried to the riverbank to strip down to his bathing suit.   Behind him were several younger men and a couple of women.   All disrobed to bathing suits and awaited the leadership of their grand marshal.

This group of polar bears waited on shore as its leader dipped his paw into the chilly water and made his way to the deeper, tumbling water.   When he plunged under, the entire celebration of polar bears rushed in to join him. They pawed and splashed their way to deeper water like cubs, trusting in their leader, eager to soak themselves in this vital experience.

Charlie, Lenny, and I stood on the shore with our families, firmly gripping the hands of our children.   We were the good parents who got their children away from the TV and outside in nature.   We brought them to this place so that they could experience the wonder of this event.   They could imagine themselves heroes crossing the treacherous winter river. Yet we held their hands to keep their imaginations from becoming consequential and to keep ourselves from becoming bad parents.

The newbie swimmers quickly turned and scurried to their towels and clothes on the shore. They claimed their victory, but they lacked Emery's endurance. They were dry and dressing when Emery lumbered out of the river and began his post-plunge routine. There was awe and applause for everyone, especially for Emery.

As we had promised, we walked to the playground behind the elementary school so Little Doug could play. On our way, he looked at me and asked, "Why did the man swim in the cold water?"

MILL RAPIDS, Ohio — Jan. 1, 2002 — Little Doug was not so little anymore. Somehow he grew taller than me. Somehow he became a freshman in college. Like me, though, he was thirsty for answers to questions, especially the *Why* questions. So he decided to follow in my footsteps and become a journalist. Of course, my footsteps would not guide him far since so much had changed in the newspaper business.   The Internet changed the way readers got their news, and the newspaper business was struggling. Little Doug would have to forge a new path through the virgin snow of technology.

One thing that hadn't changed was Emery's annual polar bear plunge. He was 95 years old now. His wife had died, but Emery still honored their wedding anniversary with a New Years Day swim in the river. This year would be a challenge, though, because Emery had broken his hip last year. He got around on a scooter now. He could stand using a cane, but he couldn't walk without help. He insisted on taking his swim, though, and his closest followers would be there to help him.

Julie, Little Doug, and I walked across River Road and past the old elementary school. The building still stood, but the school was closed, replaced by a modern school building in the newer part of town.

The approach to the river was lined with tables staffed by artists and crafters hawking their wares. Many craft pieces depicted an aurora of polar bears, a group of polar bears with the northern lights in the background. There were figurines and glasswork etched with Emery's name and official title, The Mill Rapids Polar Bear. You could buy post cards, kitchen towels, lawn ornaments, T-shirts, bathing suits, axes, and more, all with a graphic connection to Emery and his annual ritual.

Politicians, insurance agents, real estate agents, and lawyers all offered smiles, handshakes, and business cards. Among those was a CPA who had left the accounting firm he had worked for in order to start his own firm. That was Lenny. We stopped by his booth to say hello, but all we could get was a nod and a wave since he was busy touting his services to a potential new client.

None of these people were there to watch Emery swim, and none would ever swim themselves. That would be embarrassing. Reputation-killing. Who would trust a financial advisor who plunged into an icy river every year?   There was no money in that, but it attracted a crowd of spectators, and there was money in the crowd. I suppose it was no different than the newspaper business. The articles drew eyeballs, and the eyeballs drew advertisers.

We made our way to the riverside and hooked up with Charlie and Jackie.

"Where are your kids?" I asked Charlie, not that they were kids anymore.

They're here somewhere," Charlie replied.

It was futile to try to find them in the crowd. There was no way to count the number of spectators, but using the Jacobs method, I estimated there to be about 500 people.   The town had cleared vegetation along the shoreline to accommodate more people.   There was a designated area for the press, and the two local TV stations had their cameras set up there.

We could hear cheering coming from where the tables were set up, so we assumed Emery was making his entrance. "Let's get to the press area," I told Little Doug, and we headed to the roped-off area.

There was a snow-shoveled path from the table area to the riverbank, and down that path came Emery on his electric scooter. He was wrapped in a heavy blanket, and several guys in bathing suits walked alongside.   The crowd hooted and cheered as he passed by and stopped at the river's edge.

The assistants set a chair next to Emery's scooter and transferred him from the scooter to the chair, removing the blanket in the process. With a guy on each side, they lifted the chair and carried Emery into the river. They set it in the shallow water so they could gently splash Emery to acclimate him to the temperature. Then they headed to the deep area, lowered him into the swirling water, and he swam off the chair. The crowd roared.

It was not his longest swim, but it was a significant feat. His hip injury had limited his mobility, but hadn't stopped him. He got back onto the chair, and the men carefully carried him out of the water, victorious in his battle to overcome his limitation.

They quickly toweled him dry, transferred him to the scooter, re-bundled him in his blanket, and positioned him next to the press area.

Reporters tossed out their questions, and Emery answered each one like the veteran celebrity he was. Then I heard a familiar voice. Little Doug asked, "Will you do it again next year?"

"I looked forward to it all year," he replied, "but it's not as fun anymore because I need so much help. So this is my last year."

It was breaking news, news that would change New Years Day forever in Mill Rapids. I was so proud that it was my son who asked the question.

After the interviews, someone said the river was now open to any other polar bears, and a crowd of 50 flowed into the consecrated current. They weren't dammed by existential questions. They flowed freely into the icy waters without consideration of reasons or consequences. They immersed themselves in the river because it was there.

Among those daring bears were two people I knew. They weren't chickens. They were up for the challenge. They were bred from daring and confidence. From within the crowd I heard Jackie's panicked holler, "Charlie, the twins!" I looked to the river and saw the twins paddling playfully among Emery's successors.

MILL RAPIDS, Ohio — Jan. 1, 2023 — The New Years Day festivities continued after Emery retired, and for several years Emery would attend as the throng occupied the river from shore to shore. He would watch with pride from his scooter at how his simple anniversary ritual had blossomed into a community event, pulling residents away from their TV sports shows, their New Years Eve hangovers, and their cabin fevers. It was his legacy whether intended or not.

Emery died in 2008 at the age of 101. A bench was placed on the riverbank with a plaque bearing his name. That plaque was his trophy, awarded posthumously, for his years as a town idol and for 66 New Years Day swims. That plaque, a scrapbook full of newspaper articles, and some crafts bearing his name were the artifacts of his life, meager yet more than most lives collect. The greater tribute was that the event continued as an annual memorial to Emery. The artists, businessmen, and politicians staffed their tables, and a celebration of polar bears from within and outside the community would splash into the river every New Years Day.

This year was the first year I attended without the assignment to write a newspaper article. I was 65 now, the same age as Emery the first time I watched him, and I was retired. I looked back on my life as a journalist with an uneasiness. I had been an observer and reporter of people and events, a man with a camera on the riverbank, but never in the current.

It's not that I never thought about joining Emery and the other polar bears. In fact, in recent years I wore a bathing suit under my clothes just in case I got caught up in the moment, but I always returned home dry, excused myself to the bathroom, took off the bathing suit, and replaced it in the drawer without Julie seeing. Readers expected objectivity from journalists.

Now that I was retired, my thoughts turned to reminiscing, bucket lists, and the quickening of time. Maybe I would have a few years left, or maybe I would have decades. Perhaps I would reach the age of 101 like Emery. I'd probably never qualify for a bench and a plaque, and there'd be no craft items with my name on them, but I'd leave a file drawer full of by-lined articles as evidence that I was here. I had a great run as a newspaper reporter and had lots of fun chasing down answers to the five W's and an H. Those *Why* questions were tough, though.

Why did you swim, Emery? For your health? For attention? To bring the community together? I had considered all of those reasons before, and none had struck me as likely. He lived to 101, but he was not a paragon of health. He got attention, but he happily swam for decades before anyone noticed. His actions brought the community together, but that seemed more a by-product than his intention. Perhaps it was some glistening reflection in the water, some shimmering light, that got his attention and drew him in. I could never get an answer, and it drove me nuts.

I wandered around the riverbank while Julie perused the craft tables. I chatted with the folks from the TV stations as they set up their cameras. I admired Emery's bench. I stood at the river's edge and watched the torrent.

I looked back to where the elementary school once stood. It was demolished now, an empty lot where children once raised their hands to ask questions, including questions that had no answers. Over time, most of them learned and accepted the boundaries of inquiry and comfortably immersed themselves within the banks of the knowable.

People began to gather. Julie joined me with a bag of crafts she had purchased. Charlie, Jackie, Lenny, and Doris joined us. The high school marching band played a couple of songs. I held Julie's hand as the mayor stepped in front of the crowd with his microphone.

He welcomed the swimmers and the spectators. He thanked the businesses for their participation. He thanked his fellow council members. He thanked the fire department and paramedics for being there. Then he recited Emery's story.

I began to grow nervous as his speech progressed. My heartbeat accelerated. As he wound down his address, I gave Julie's hand a squeeze, then let it go.

"And now," the mayor declared, "in the memory of Emery Adams, the river is open to all polar bears!"

The crowd rushed toward the water. Men and women, young and old. All in their bathing suits, and some in costumes of various genres.

Once the crowd was in, I took a few steps forward and dropped my coat and sweater. A few more steps and kicked off my shoes. Then I dropped my pants and continued toward the water in only my bathing suit.

"What are you doing!?" Julie screamed at me.

I continued over the snow to the water, stepping onto the smooth cold of the limestone riverbed, and without hesitation, I threw myself into the deeper water. I rolled to my back and looked to shore. I could see Julie's panicked face, her mittened hands covering her open mouth. Lenny was shaking his head. Charlie raised his hands above his head and clapped, a huge smile on his face.

I was no longer a journalist. I had no deadlines, no writing rules, no expectations of objectivity to meet. I was free from that role. Free to be an old man driven crazy searching for answers to unanswerable questions.

Then it all became a blur. My chest was painfully tight, my body frozen. I was vaguely aware of people pulling on my arms, dragging me out of the water and onto the shore. The next thing I remembered was waking up in the hospital. Someone told me that I had suffered a heart attack, but that I'd be OK.

Julie was at my bedside holding my hand. She kissed me and said she loved me. I said I loved her, too. She said I was lucky to be alive. I could have drowned. My body could have been washed to Lake Erie. She said it was fortunate that so many other swimmers were there to pull me to shore.

"Why did you do it?" she asked.

I pondered her question, wanting to give her a good answer, some logical reason for the risk I took. I wanted to give her profound words that would explain my actions, but I was never good with *Why* questions. There was no better answer than the one Emery gave me.

"Because I'm nuts?" I replied.

The Internship Report

On December 15, 1978, I completed my computer science internship. I thank the university, our distinguished dean, and all of my outstanding professors for making this internship possible.

As required, I am writing this internship report to receive college credit toward my degree next year. Typically, an internship report would include a description of the company, a description of my responsibilities, details of projects I completed, and a summary of what I learned.

Regrettably, I cannot provide all of the information required. The company was a defense contractor, and as such, security and confidentiality were paramount. On my first day, they admonished me to never disclose the company name, its address, the fact that I worked there, or anything about its products or projects. So in this report, I'll provide an account of just those activities that I can discuss.

On my first day, I parked my blue, 1972 Ford Maverick in the parking lot in front of the imposing building. I could not have been more confident about my computer knowledge and programming skills. The university prepared me well in that regard, but as I watched the swarm of employees flow into the facility, nerves turned my stomach.

I was an intern, a prestigious rank among my college classmates, but the bottom of the pecking order among company workers. I feared this would be as horrible as my first days as a Boy Scout when I was working toward the rank of tenderfoot. Camping experience was a requirement, and on my first camping trip, the more senior scouts had sent me and another newbie to the camp office to borrow a left-handed smoke shifter. I recalled the laughter from that prank as I sat in the parking lot.

Not wanting to experience that kind of initiation again, I started the Maverick, backed out of the parking space, and headed toward the exit. Then I thought about the heckling I would get from my classmates for wimping out, so I circled back and re-parked the car.

Another wave of apprehension passed through me as I fretted about not fitting in. Like the time I was turned away at the door of a disco, unaware that the jeans I was wearing violated their dress code. I was an expert in programming, but had no idea about office protocol and how I would get things done in this strange environment.

I started the car again and shifted it into reverse. Then I realized that I was wearing a suit and tie, the proper costume for this venue, so all I had to do was act the part. Ad-lib my lines. Become my character. Break a leg. I put the car in park and turned off the engine. I opened the door and marched to the lobby as if I were a seasoned employee. Like Oliver from *The Man in the Dog Suit*, I put on my dog suit and became a bold and confident staff member.

I went to the lobby, and a receptionist named Mary set me up. I didn't know if her name was Mary, that's just what I called her. I introduced myself and asked what her name was, and she gave me a cold stare while dialing a number on the phone. "Mary" seemed like a sweet, respectable name. I thought it fit her well despite the fact that she wore a uniform and carried a gun.

She called another guard, a big burly guy, and had me go to another room with him. It was equipped with a camera, and he took two photos of me for my badge. I was smiling in one and more stern-faced in the other. He threw away the smiling photo. "If you're ever interrogated by the Soviets, you don't want a smiley photo," he explained. "They'll see you as weak."

"That makes sense," I mumbled, wondering if he was serious.

He laminated my badge, which included my photo and a number, but no name. "You don't want the enemy to know your name," he said.

"Right," I agreed, now curious about how many employees had been subject to Soviet interrogation, but not wanting to ask in case it turned out to be a prank on his part.

He explained that when entering the building, I should show it to the guard, and the guard was required to tap it with their finger. He also explained that I must open my briefcase for the guard whenever entering or leaving the building.

"What if I don't have a briefcase?" I asked.

"Everyone carries a briefcase," he replied.

I immediately felt naked on stage without this essential prop, so I made a mental note to buy a nice briefcase on my way home from work that day.

Once I got my badge, Mary called my manager who came to the lobby to show me the way to the department.

"It's great to have you onboard," Herman, my manager, said. "You bring strong skills, and we have lots of work lined up for you."

"I'm looking forward to it," I replied, trying my best to cover up my trepidation.

We headed into the main hall and turned left down a long corridor. We came to the end, and to the right were double doors and a window into another lobby. I looked through the window and Herman explained, "This part of the building is where the aeronautical engineers work. They are one of the two customers of our Data Processing Department."

The lobby was well-appointed with carpet, potted ferns, spotlights illuminating fine artwork on the walls, and a young, attractive woman at a mahogany reception desk.

"Who is the other customer?" I asked.

"That would be Headquarters in California. We have two teams of programmers. You are in the Engineering Programming Team, which develops software that these guys use to design their products. The other team is the Business Programming Team, which develops software to create business reports for Headquarters."

I was anxious to step through the double doors into the lush lobby, but Herman led us the other way. "Data Processing is over here."   We walked through what looked like an exterior door, and stepped down into a thin-walled hallway with the ambience of a mobile home. "The Data Processing area is an addition to the original building. They added modular units for the computer and our staff."

That was nice of them, I thought. It wasn't plush like the aeronautical engineering area, but it was clean and there was a roof over our heads.

Herman led me though a door into the computer room. We stepped up to a counter and surveyed the equipment beyond.   I was reassured when I saw a familiar sight, an IBM 370 on a table in the middle of the room.   A stack of plastic buckets sat on top of it, an operator console to the left, disk and tape drives to the rear, and line printers to the right.

A computer operator pushed a stack of green and white computer printouts across the counter to Herman. "Here are some printouts for your folks," she said. Herman introduced me and explained that this is where I would pick up printouts for my programming tasks.

The next door down was a break room with a refrigerator, coffee machines, microwave, and a few tables and chairs. Beyond the break room was a small supply room. It had a few storage cabinets with office supplies, and in the back, a guy was installing an office system and printer. Herman introduced me to Dennis, the systems programmer that kept our computers running.

"Welcome," the curly-haired, wide-eyed Dennis said, "And meet the 6640! She's our new inkjet printer, part of this new office system. It's a whole new printing technology that squirts ink at the paper rather than impacting the paper. Tiny drops of black ink are guided by an electromagnetic field to form characters. It produces beautiful printing. It's going to change everything about the way we produce printed material. It's an amazing printer! Absolutely amazing!"

"Wow. Amazing," I said, thinking he was overacting his part. I wondered why he was so excited about a printer. I wondered why I should feel so excited. Weren't impact printers sufficient for putting ink onto paper? Wasn't a solid strike of a hammer against an inked ribbon the pinnacle of printing technology? Why is an inkjet printer any better? Dennis made it sound as significant as the invention of the transistor. I was skeptical, but his excitement did arouse a certain feeling of fascination within me, a certain feeling of privilege to work in the presence of new and different technology.

Herman and I continued down the hallway to the last door on the left, which opened into the Data Processing offices. Herman's office was by the entrance, and two rows of cubicles filled the rest of the room. To the left were cubicles for the Engineering Programming Team, identified by a sign hanging from the suspended acoustic ceiling. To the right were cubicles for the Business Programming Team. It was also identified with a hanging sign, but stapled to that sign were multiple cruise missiles, not real ones, but golden paper cutouts.

Herman took me around to meet everyone. On my team were Ed and Martha. Ed was recently hired and appeared to be in his 40s. He was clean-shaven, had a precision haircut, and wore a three-piece suit. His cubicle was immaculate; the only item on his desk was a three-inch binder containing the employee handbook.

"Ed used to be a vehicle inspector for the state," Herman explained.

"Impressive," I responded as if that were top-tier experience for a computer programmer.

Martha was a year older than me at 22. I would soon turn 21. She was a recent computer science graduate from the university I attended. She was gorgeous, with blonde hair down to her shoulders, light complexion, green eyes, tall, and wearing a short skirt. I learned that she was a jogger and a weight-lifter. Maybe she was out of my league, but still, I noted that there was no ring on her finger.

"Martha will be your mentor," Herman said.

"Great!" I replied. I was particularly excited about that, much more excited than I was about the inkjet printer.

The business team programmers were Curtis, Howard, and Jeannie. Curtis was 30-something, tall, skinny, with short, receding, blonde hair, and a three-piece suit.

"Derek!" he shouted expressively as we approached. "Great to see you!"

Did we meet before? No. Were we best buddies from the past? No. That's just the way Curtis spoke. He could make anyone feel welcome.

"They call me Crazy Curtis," he said. "Some just call me Crazy."

Howard was from a different generation. He was in his 60s and wore brown. Brown shoes, brown socks, brown slacks, brown shirt, brown tie, and brown suit jacket. A brown fedora hung on a hook in his cubicle. On the wall above his desk was a sepia photo of Captain Grace Hopper in her Navy uniform in front of a PDP-11 computer. Grace was his hero, presumably for her role in developing the COBOL programming language, Howard's area of expertise.

Jeannie was in her 30s, short and fit with hair shorter than mine. She had the handshake of a wrestler and eyes that burned with determination. A purple, white, and golden ribbon hung on her coat hook, a memento from her recent participation in an Equal Rights Amendment march. I made a mental note not to make her angry or get into an arm-wrestling match with her.

My cubicle was between Martha's and Ed's. I spent that first day with Martha, who showed me how to access the mainframe via the computer terminals, which were located in a room off of the cubicle area. She introduced me to the computer program that I was to work on. It was top secret, so I can't go into details, but it involved FORTRAN programming.

Martha's knowledge was impressive. She thoroughly understood the programming environment and the project, and she had a clear and concise communication style. It helped me focus on the topic, and it kept me somewhat undistracted by her long, shapely legs and short skirt.

After a few days, I was on a roll. Every day, I'd say good morning to Mary and open my briefcase for her to inspect. It was empty except for a peanut butter sandwich, a bag of chips, and a Tab pop.

"Tab causes cancer," she would tell me.

"Only if you're a lab rat," I would respond.

Then she'd tap my badge and let me pass.

In the evening, I would open my briefcase, and in addition to checking it, she would ask, "Do you have any confidential information?"

"Let me check," I'd respond. I'd take a close look at the empty briefcase. "Nope, no confidential information here."

She would laugh, and I would leave with a comfortable feeling about work. She was much warmer than I had first thought, especially at the end of the day, and never did she point her gun at me.

On Friday, it was raining. Water was dripping from the ceiling throughout the cubicle area. One of those leaks was above my cubicle. Herman distributed plastic buckets to the team. He gave me two, one to put under the leak, and another to put under the leak while I was emptying the first. Herman was a great manager, always prepared for unexpected events like this.

That afternoon, it was quiet in the cubicles. Everyone was at their desks reading their FORTRAN or COBOL listings. The only sound was the steady drip of rainwater into the buckets. Then the silence was broken by Crazy Curtis who hollered, "Fire!" at the top of his lungs.

I thought the building was on fire, but rubber bands were flying in the air. One landed on my head. Then I heard Martha say, "I'm hit." Then Ed said, "I'm hit."

I stood up, and Curtis, Howard, and Jeannie launched more rubber bands at me. "You're hit," Jeannie declared. "When you get hit by a rubber band, you're supposed to say 'I'm hit.'"

"OK, I'm hit. I didn't know."

It turned out that every Friday, sometime between 1:00 and 5:00 PM, a rubber band battle would occur between the two teams. The team who had at least one surviving player would win a golden cruise missile to staple to their department sign.

Our department had no cruise missiles. Martha said it was because of Snooty Trudy. Snooty was a college professor on sabbatical from another university, not mine, and had worked here on contract to gain real-world experience. According to Martha, she didn't mix well with the other programmers. She was opposed to the ERA and went out of her way to engage Jeannie in passionate arguments. She didn't think it lady-like for

Grace Hopper to join the Navy, offending Howard. She didn't like Martha's short skirts, and she didn't like the rubber band battles that Crazy Curtis started. Consequently, our team had no victories, and the job didn't work out for Snooty.

The next week, I had an important meeting with one of the aeronautical engineers to go over some of the mathematical formulas he had provided for my project. He went by the name "Bashful." Jeannie knew him from hallway arguments about the ERA. She explained that "Bashful" was his pilot call sign when he was in the Air Force, and call signs were usually demeaning or rooted in some personality weakness. Bashful was actually extremely forward and arrogant, she warned me.

So I had mixed feelings about the meeting, but I headed to the plush lobby and said hello to the lady at the reception desk. "I have an appointment with Bashful," I said. "I hope he won't feel diffident about meeting with me." She smiled and dialed him up. Shortly, he blasted through the door like a missile from a silo to escort me to his office.

All of the aeronautical engineers had private offices with doors that closed, many with windows that looked out onto the lawn or into the landscaped atrium. The area was adorned with photos of aircraft and missiles, potted plants, and an indoor waterfall. To top it off, there were no leaks in the ceiling.

Bashful gave me a firm handshake with a grip almost as strong as Jeannie's. He led me to his office and directed me to a chair. As Jeannie had described, he was arrogant. Everything he said was tinged with insult, like: *You probably don't understand mathematics*, and *I don't expect that you're going to get this right.*

I pointed him to one of the mathematical formulas he had provided and I said, "You know, I think there's something wrong with this equation. I can't put my finger on it since I don't know math, but it just looks catawampus, so I wanted to run it past you."

He studied the formula silently for quite awhile. I worried that I might have been mistaken about the formula. Maybe it was just fine. Or maybe I was right, and he just needed some time to figure out how to deflect blame.

"Somebody really screwed this up," he declared. He made corrections with his pencil and handed it back to me. "I don't know how this place will survive when I retire."

"Thank you," I said, and I got up to leave. He walked me to the door, as he was required to do.

"When are you going to be done with this?" he asked.

"I don't know, this is just my second week."

"Well, let's not putz around."

Motivated by those inspiring words, I went back to my cubicle, my mission completed successfully. I was beginning to feel a little more confident in my role.

I pondered in my office about my role in the department and how best to fit in. I didn't want to follow in the path of Snooty Trudy. I came up with an idea. I took out my FORTRAN coding sheet and penciled out a small program. I went to the terminal room. After a little editing and debugging, I had the program working.

Then I needed some data. I walked around the cubicle area and chatted with Crazy Curtis and Jeannie. Howard was on the phone with Headquarters. He spent many hours talking to them about their requests for different types of reports. Anyway, while I was chatting and wandering, I was estimating distances between cubicles and the heights of cubicle walls.

I went back to the terminal room and entered my estimates as data to my program. The results seemed reasonable, but I had to figure out how to print them. If I sent them to the line printer in the computer room, the operator would see them, and this information was top secret. With a little effort, I figured out how to print them on the new inkjet printer in the supply room, then rushed there to retrieve them. The output was beautiful, crisp type on virgin paper never touched by an impact printer head.

While in the supply room, I stole three protractors, three slide rules, and some paper clips. I was able to quickly fashion three rubber band launchers out of those materials. Then I just needed a top secret meeting with Martha and Ed.

We met in the conference room next to Herman's office, and we closed the blinds for privacy. I gave them each a rubber band launcher and a printout.

"These printouts are customized for each of us," I explained. "They are range tables that give you the launch angle for each of our targets, Curtis, Howard, and

Jeannie. And they tell you how far to pull back the rubber band. So you hold the launcher by the slide rule, then set the protractor to the specified angle, load the rubber band on the protractor, pull it back the specified distance, and let it rip."

So at our agreed upon time on Friday afternoon, we launched our attack and listened for the results. *I'm hit, I'm hit,* and *I'm hit* declared Curtis, Howard, and Jeannie. We had won our first battle. Martha took receipt of our first golden missile. It was exciting, for more than one reason, to watch Martha step onto a chair and staple our first golden missile to our department sign.

The next morning I pulled into the parking lot and I noticed an identical Maverick parked at an angle across two spaces. I parked next to it as its driver was getting out, and I could see that it was Ed.

"Good morning, Ed," I called. Is this your car?"

"Good morning. Yes, this is my baby. You have one, too!"

"Yes, it's been a good car. Got me through college."

"I bought mine new in 1972," he said.

"It's in great condition," I noted. "No rust."

"I take good care of her. I've got the Chilton's repair and tune-up guide so I can do much of the maintenance myself."

Ed reached into his pocket and pulled out a penny. He walked around my Maverick, sticking the penny into the tread of each of my tires. "Looks like you've got plenty of wear left on your tires. You always want to check that for safety purposes."

"Thanks," I said.

He was starting to check the condition of my windshield wipers when we heard the squealing of tires. It was Curtis in his brand new Lincoln Continental Town Car. It was a huge car, but Curtis drove it like a sports cars. He pulled up next to us, taking up four parking spaces. It was a beautiful car, tan with shiny chrome, the Lincoln hood ornament out front, oval opera windows in the rear, and leather seats inside.

Ed and I both felt out-classed as we salivated over his car. I resolved to save money for the day I'd trade in my Maverick for a Lincoln, or maybe something even better. Something bigger, something shinier, something faster. I realized that you can't be satisfied with what you have forever; you must always strive for better.

The three of us walked into the lobby. Mary coldly inspected Curtis's briefcase and tapped his badge. Then she did Ed. Then I stepped up.

"Good morning, Mary," I said.

"Good morning, Derek," she said with a warm smile. She thoroughly inspected my briefcase, which was empty except for my lunch. Then she tapped my badge. "Have a great day!"

Inside, Curtis and Ed were incredulous. "How do you get a smile out of her?" Curtis asked.

"How do you know her name?" Ed inquired. "According to the employee handbook, guards aren't supposed to reveal their names."

I just shrugged my shoulders.

As we headed down the hall, Curtis pulled out his badge. "Look at this," he said. "I've been using this for almost a year."

I looked at the photo on his badge, then looked at Curtis. There was no resemblance. Crazy Curtis had taped a photo of Koko the gorilla over his photo. Koko was the gorilla that could communicate using sign language, the one who, using a camera and a mirror, took his own self-portrait for the cover of *National Geographic* magazine.

"That's crazy," I said, and he immediately replied, "No, that's Koko."

I grabbed a cup of coffee and settled into my cubicle. My first priority of the day was to call Maintenance about the flickering florescent tube above my cubicle. It had been flickering since my first day. I had reported it several times, and so had Herman, but it still was not fixed.

I dialed the extension, which I knew by heart now, and spoke to the administrator. She reassured me that my request had not been lost or forgotten. It was on their priority list, and they would get to it as soon as it rose to the top of the list.

She explained in her empathetic, almost sensual, voice that they had limited resources and that service requests for the modular addition were second priority to the main building. I had intended a verbal fit of rage, but her voice was so caring, so seductively convincing, and so erotically alluring, that I said thank you and hung up.

Then I felt a wave of jealousy as I pictured her on Bashful's lap in his elegantly illuminated luxury suite.

I had reached a point in my project that required a new piece of equipment. Herman had ordered it, and now Dennis was installing it in the terminal room. It was a Tektronix 4014 graphics terminal. It consisted of a terminal screen and a keyboard atop a pedestal. The 4014 would allow an aeronautical engineer to see a line drawing of a component they were designing.

"This is amazing technology!" Dennis exclaimed as I watched him install the unit. "It uses a direct-view bistable storage tube. It uses two electron beams, a flood gun and a writing gun, to store a complex drawing on the screen. The image doesn't have to be refreshed like it does on a cathode-ray tube. I mean, you are a lucky duck to be able to swim in this pond. This is absolutely amazing technology!"

Suddenly, I didn't feel so bad about the flickering florescent tube. I was going to be swimming in a pond with this amazing electrical device.

In the weeks that followed, I played with the 4014, writing programs to display various lines and curves and geometrical shapes. As part of my self-training, I embarked on an effort to program some computer art, and soon I completed a picture of a naked woman. With some tweaking of parameters, the curves were sensually smooth and alluring. With the click of a key, you could switch from a back view to a profile view, and from a profile view to a frontal view.

With my self-training complete, I turned my attention back to my assigned project, but word had gotten around about my computer artwork. Bashful paid a rare visit to our terminal room while I was working there. The rest of my coworkers and Herman crowded into the room, curious about what was happening.

"Show me the naked woman," Bashful insisted.

I was in trouble now, I thought. My hands were shaky as I launched the program, my face red as the image displayed, my voice brittle as I explained how to move from one view to another.

"How did you create this?" he asked.

"Just some FORTRAN programming," I answered.

"Where did you get the mathematical formulas for these curves?"

"I figured them out," I replied.

"This is good work. Give me the formulas."

I thought about it for a moment, then said, "What do I get in exchange?"

Bashful didn't hesitate, "What do you want?"

"Hmmm. I'll have to think about that," I said.

"Call me," he directed, then turned to Herman. "This guy is good. Keep him." Then he marched off.

When he was gone, most of the department applauded me, except for Jeannie. Her eyes were still fixed on the screen image. I hoped I hadn't made her angry.

I waited a couple of days, then called Bashful to propose a deal. I said I'd give him the formulas if he would call Maintenance and submit a service request for us. The request was for repair of the leaky roof and replacement of all florescent light bulbs in the modular addition. He agreed. Workers started the next day.

By late fall, I was done with the programming project and turned my attention to documentation. I had turned 21 by then, and my coworkers picked a Friday evening after work to take me to Carnival Bill's Lounge to celebrate. It was in the neighborhood, and all six of us could fit comfortably in Curtis's Lincoln.

We were ready to go, except Howard was stuck on the phone with Headquarters in California. They wanted a new option on an employee report, and Howard was in heated debate with the person on the phone. Finally, he relented and hung up.

"Can you believe that?" he lamented. "These corporate bureaucrats want an option to sort the employee report by middle initial! Why would anyone need that?"

"Howard, you need a drink. Let's go," said Curtis.

Carnival Bill's was a popular bar owned and operated by Carnival Bill himself. Whether he ever worked in a carnival was unclear, but the lounge had a calliope that played lively circus music. That provided good entertainment during times when there was no live band, but the best entertainment was when Carnival Bill played the piano. He and Curtis were good friends. They were a lot alike, both flamboyant and a little crazy.

We got a table for six in the middle of the room near the small stage and piano. Quite a few other small groups were already seated as local workers were getting off work, and there were a number of people perched on stools at the bar.

After our drinks arrived, Crazy Curtis stepped onto the stage, lifted the microphone out of its stand, and turned it on. Faster than Dr. Banner could transform into the Incredible Hulk, Curtis transformed into an emcee.

"Welcome, everyone, to Carnival Bill's Lounge," he announced. "How are you all doing this evening?"

Cheers arose.

"I'd like to direct your attention to the fine group of people sitting here in the center ring. These are the finest coworkers anyone could ever ask for, and we have a special occasion to celebrate. Derek, here, recently turned 21, and he's here to reap the rewards of his milestone. Stand up, Derek."

I stood up, a little red in the face, then even redder as cheers and applause rattled the room. I got the feeling that Crazy Curtis was not a stranger to these folks.

"Are there any other birthdays in the house?"

People at another table started pointing at a woman at their table. She slumped down in her chair, but meekly raised her hand. Curtis walked over to her, "Happy birthday. What is your name?"

"Margaret," she answered into the microphone.

"And what milestone did you reach?"

She didn't want to answer, but her friends answered for her, "Forty!"

"Congratulations, Margaret! And what would make your day special?"

She shrugged her shoulders, not sure how to answer. "I don't know. A free drink?"

"Waitress, can we get a free drink for Margaret?"

The waitress filled a margarita glass and brought it to her. She took a sip, and Curtis asked, "What is it?"

"It's water," she laughed.

"It's water, ladies and gentlemen! And it's free here at Carnival Bill's Lounge!" Curtis continued, "So if we can get Carnival Bill to come to the piano, we'll sing "Happy Birthday" to Margaret and Derek."

They completed a round of "Happy Birthday." Then Curtis asked, "Now what do we want Carnival Bill to do?"

The crowd had heard it before. They didn't hesitate. In unison, they responded, "Sing us a song!"

"What do we want him to do?" Curtis asked again.

"Sing us a song!"

"I can't hear you!"

"Sing us a song!!"

Curtis returned the microphone to the stand by the piano, and Carnival Bill rattled the keys to Billy Joel's "Piano Man." He'd sing a verse about someone with an unfulfilled dream, and when he got to the refrain, "Sing us a song," the whole crowd joined in.

I sipped on my margarita as Bill sang the song. By the time he was done, my drink was done, too, and the waitress refreshed me.

"That was quite a show," Ed said to Curtis. "You should be a professional emcee."

"Actually," Curtis smiled, "I always wanted to be a game show host or a comedian. Here, I ended up being a COBOL programmer."

Howard chimed in, "You're still young. There's time. Don't let yourself get to be an old man like me without doing what you really want to do."

"Have you done everything you wanted to do, Howard?" Curtis asked.

"You never stop wanting to do things. I look at Grace Hopper, and she just keeps on ticking. She retires, then she goes back to active duty. The more things you do, the more things you want to do. For me, I'd like to teach programming after I'm done here. What about the rest of you? What are your dreams?"

"My dream is women's rights and equality," Jeannie offered. "It doesn't have much to do with computers, but that's what matters most to me."

"For me, the dream has always been about safety and security," Ed said. "Coming here is a chance to do that on a larger scale than vehicle inspections. It's a chance to make the world more secure."

Martha chimed in, "I love what I'm doing here, but I also want to get married and raise a family. I really want to be a mom."

"You'd be a great mom," Howard said. "And what about you, Derek?"

I could feel redness spread over my face. I hadn't thought in terms of dreams. It was more about having a job and an income. I loved programming, and I was good at it. It was satisfying to get a program debugged and running correctly. It's what I wanted to do, but why? If this was the role I was going to play, shouldn't it be for some meaningful purpose? For some dream that I have, or should have, for my life?   I shook my head and admitted, "I don't really know what my dream is yet, but I love programming."

"You're on the right track, and you'll discover a dream or two as you move forward," Howard assured me. "None of us will become "Piano Man" characters."

December 15 arrived. Not only was it my last day, but Martha was hosting a holiday party at her apartment after work. I spent the day turning over my project files. As 5:00 PM approached, my coworkers surrounded my cubicle and presented me with a going away card. Reading their notes was touching. *You have a future in weapons design.   Thanks for showing me the light. Umbrella for sale. I hope to see more of your artwork.* Surprisingly, that last one was signed "Jeannie."

It felt good to look up at our team's sign and see all of the cruise missiles, almost as many as the other team had. It felt good knowing that I was leaving the team with better lighting and the ability to look up without getting splashed in the face. And, although I resented his arrogance, it was good to know that I had earned a degree of respect from Bashful.

"It's five," Martha said. "Let's party."

I put the farewell card into my briefcase. On the way out of the lobby, I opened my briefcase for Mary. "Do you have any confidential information?" she asked.

"No," I said. "Just a going-away card."

She picked up my card to take a look. "I need to collect your badge."

I handed her my badge.

"That's a nice card," she said. "They're a nice group of people." She put the card back into my briefcase along with a flyer. "This is a schedule for a little band I'm in. We play in local bars. Come and see us sometime."

"I'll do that," I said. Once again, I left with a comfortable feeling about this place, and for the first time, I left with something in my briefcase.

I arrived at Martha's apartment. She took my coat and put it on the bed in her bedroom. On the dining table were sandwiches and meatballs, chips and dip, salads and vegetables, and cookies and candy. And lots of alcohol. Curtis was at the kitchen counter pouring wine and mixing drinks.

"How about a White Russian?" Curtis hawked to me.

"Sure," I said, having no idea what that was.

He mixed it as if he had tended bar all of his life. "Just so you know, this uses genuine, imported Russian vodka."

"Totally appropriate for this group," I said, and I was hooked when I took my first sip.

After a few more, the evening spun like ice cubes in an old fashioned glass, stirring the music, the stories, the food, and the laughter into a smooth and pleasurable blend. I sat next to Martha on the couch. She was still in her short, black skirt. She was drinking at the same rapid pace as me. She got up and brought us another round, and when she sat down next to me again, she took my hand in hers. "I really enjoyed working with you," she said.

As the party wound down, I went to the bedroom to get my coat. Martha joined me and shut the door. Without saying anything, she put her arms around my neck. She pulled me close. I put my arms around her waist, and we passionately kissed. She was such a good mentor.

She slipped a paper containing her phone number into my shirt pocket and handed me my coat. I said goodnight and headed to my car more excited, more confident, and more hopeful than ever before.

I inserted a Billy Joel 8-track and pulled onto the road. I made my way home through the vodka-laced fog and got the car into the garage without ripping off either mirror or driving through the back wall, then I stumbled to my room.

I opened my briefcase and reread my card. *Keep in touch*, Martha had written. Then I looked at the flyer Mary had given me. It had a picture of the band members captioned with their names. The name corresponding to Mary's photo was, indeed, Mary.

I rolled a piece of paper into the typewriter and composed this internship report. I learned so much from this internship, most of which had nothing to do with computer programming. I learned how to project confidence when my feet were trembling in my boots. I learned not to be a Snooty Trudy, and how much fun it was to embrace the craziness of my colleagues. I learned a little about negotiating, too.

As I looked over my internship report, I realized one other thing. I had always been satisfied with the quality of a typewritten page, but now the harsh hammering, raucous rattling, and patchy printing seemed barbaric compared to the refined elegance of an inkjet printer. Like a clunky Maverick compared to a luxurious Lincoln. Suddenly, the world seemed full of improvement opportunities. I still don't know specifically what my dream will be and how I will use my programming skills, but this internship ignited within me a passion to make things better, more elegant, and more suitable for humankind.

River Rats

The River Rats Marine Company was a family business located just above the dam near Locksville, Ohio. It was a landmark along the river, an institution, an integral part of the history of northwest Ohio. In May of 1979, though, its future was in question.

The company was started by the late Robert Hargan in the early 1920s. He started by building runabouts that used early outboard motors like the Evinrude. He grew the business to become the predominant boat sales and repair company in the area.

His son, Eugene, took over the business and continued to grow it, adding a marina, an RV park, and an RV storage facility to the property. Eugene, his wife, Ellie, and their son, Trey, were proud to be known as the River Rats.

The Monday evening dinner conversation centered around preparations for the Memorial Day weekend. The boat shop mechanics were working extra hours to ready customers' vessels for the summer season. The sales department was expediting deliveries so buyers could take their maiden voyages over the holiday weekend. Seasonal campers were moving their recreational vehicles onto sites in the RV park. Customers who kept their house trailers and boats at River Rat RV Storage were requesting that their RVs be moved to their sites and that their boats be launched and docked at their slips. Preparations were underway for the Memorial Day barbecue and dance, an annual summer kickoff complete with food, music, and dancing.

It was a busy time of year, and there was still work to be done that evening, so the Hargans rushed through dinner. Before anyone left the table, though, Ellie retrieved an envelope that had come in the mail. "This letter came for you," she said as she handed it to Trey. "It's from Cincinnati."

Shop talk stopped. Eugene, Ellie, and Trey knew what the letter was about.

Trey was a business major at the university and would graduate in a couple of weeks. He had been interviewing for marketing communication positions at several companies, including Datafoil Consulting in Cincinnati. Trey began the job search as an exercise of due diligence, scouting trips to reassure himself that the family business was his best fit. The expectation had always been that Trey would take over the River Rat business, but after a few interviews, he was becoming intrigued with those career prospects.

Trey nervously tore open the envelope. If it was a rejection letter, the waters ahead would be straight and easy to navigate. If it was an offer letter, he'd face a fork in the river and would have to navigate left or right.

"What does it say?" Ellie asked.

Trey handed it to his dad. "They offered me the job," he said blandly.

Eugene read the letter silently, then set it down on the table and laid a finger on one part. "Holy crap," he said. "They're offering you a fortune."

Ellie picked up the letter, read it, and with a smile said, "Congratulations."

"They want an answer in two weeks," Trey said.

"Remember what your grandfather used to say. The best boss to work for is yourself," Eugene said.

Ellie put her hand on Eugene's to preempt any debate. "You just need to think it through and do what's best for you," she advised. That was the same advice she had given when Trey was considering enrolling in college. He had reasoned that a college business degree would better equip him to take over and manage River Rat Marine. His dad had agreed.

Trey nodded. It all seemed so real and so fast. "Well, I need to finish the newsletter," he said as he stood up. Trey headed to the office next door to their house, and Eugene headed to the tractor to move house trailers from storage to their campsites.

Trey moored himself to the typewriter. He had one more short article to write, then he could drop off his packet for typesetting in the morning. The *River Rat*

Rag was a monthly, tabloid-size newspaper that was sent to their boat customers, storage customers, and seasonal campers. It was filled with advice about boat operation and maintenance, fishing information, and social events at the RV park. It also profiled some long-term customers of the business.

The publication was Trey's brainchild, his major contribution to the River Rats dynasty. It kept their customers informed and engaged, and free copies available to the public lured others to boating and camping. Its costs were paid by advertisers, mostly local businesses like the sporting goods store, grocery store, and eateries. Major boat brands sold and serviced by River Rat Marine also bought ads. The newsletter had a positive impact on the bottom line of the business. Trey was proud of his success, as was Eugene. It boded well for his success when it came time for Trey to captain the company.

The *Rag* was Trey's favorite responsibility. It was the one job that sparkled brighter than any other. He performed other duties. He changed oil and tuned outboard motors. He replaced shear pins. He repaired damaged fiberglass. He launched boats and hauled trailers. He sold boats and equipment, touting the features and benefits of various product lines and negotiating mutually beneficial deals. But none of those tasks matched the satisfaction he got from writing the *Rag.* That was his passion, his niche, his calling. That's what led him to focus on marketing communication at school, and that's the position Datafoil was offering him.

Trey pushed the job offer out of his mind while he worked the typewriter keys. His words flowed like a river onto the page. When he finished, he pulled the page from the roller, made a few edits with a red pen, and added the page to the folder he would take to the typesetter.

With that task complete, he sat back in his chair and looked out the window to the entrance of the River Rat property. There, along the main highway, propped up on blocks, was the old *River Rat I,* a 20-foot wooden runabout built by his late grandfather. It served as a billboard for the business, but for Trey it brought a tangled sense of pride and guilt.

When he was 15, Eugene had asked him to bring the *River Rat I* from its slip along the river to the boat launch. A spring storm was coming, so the current was strong and the winds gusty as he backed the boat out of its slip. Trey was a skilled boatman for his age; nonetheless, as he eased it downstream and turned starboard into the inlet toward the launch, the current and the wind wrested control from him. The stern swung to port and crashed into rocks at the inlet entrance. The wooden hull cracked, and his grandfather's treasure came to rest on the bottom of the shallow inlet.

The accident had not only flooded the boat, but had flooded Trey's soul with sorrow and guilt. It had drowned his confidence.

The accident had thrown Eugene into a whirlpool of emotion, furiously angry, numb with grief over the loss of his father's endowment. All of those emotions had rained down on Trey. *Just go do something else,* Eugene had snapped when Trey had tried to help him extricate the boat from the inlet. *Go do your schoolwork.* Eugene, alone, had rigged straps around the damaged vessel, had lifted it using the old crane that he used to dredge the inlets, and had moved it to the property entrance.

In time, the current of emotions had calmed, the winds of anger had stilled. Eugene had apologized to Trey for his words and had taken the blame for the accident. *It wasn't your fault*, Eugene had told him. *I should have gone with you given the conditions.*

As Trey looked out the office window, he felt pride for his grandfather and sorrow for his mistake. No matter how many times his father had repeated *It wasn't your fault*, Trey's guilt and sorrow persisted.

Eugene backed the tractor to the tongue of a house trailer in the RV storage building. He hitched it to the tractor, then eased it out of its parking space and out of the building. As he headed down the gravel road toward the RV sites, he passed the old boat at the property entrance. Whenever he passed the old boat, he could feel his father's presence. When the business was going well, he could feel the warmth of his father's pride. When there were business challenges, he could hear his father asking, *How are you going to deal with this?*

That's the question that vexed Eugene as he passed the boat and headed to the RV site. He had supported Trey's desire to go to college. It would make him a better leader for the business. He had supported him interviewing for other positions, convinced that doing so would prove the family business to be a better path for Trey, but seeing

Datafoil's salary offer alarmed him. *How dare they entice him with money*, he thought.

He thought about those days when Robert was at the company's helm, Eugene was planning the RV park, and Trey was a young prince playing with his toys. Down by thc boat launch, Trey would dig channels into the shoreline for his toy boats and would scrape roads into the dirt for his toy trucks. Trey would even make an RV park with roads and trailer sites for his customers. Those memories brought Eugene hope that the River Rat life was in Trey's blood.

Eugene positioned the trailer in its site, then unhitched it from the tractor. The sun was orange in the west, so Eugene drove to the marina knowing that Ellie would be there. They would often end long workdays watching the sunset from the dock.

He sat next to her on the dock, their legs dangling over the side, and he took her hand.

"Did you get everything done today?" she asked. That was the usual question during these busy times.

"No," he replied. That was the usual answer.

"There's always tomorrow."

"I hope so," Eugene said. "I hope we don't lose Trey."

Ellie put her arm around Eugene and rubbed his back. "We aren't going to lose Trey. He will always be our son regardless of what he decides to do."

"Yeah, I know," Eugene mumbled. It wasn't the first time Ellie gently reminded him that business and family were separate things. "In a way, it might be foolish for him not to take that job. It's good money."

"It is," Ellie replied, but she wanted to say that it should not be about the money. She wanted to say that Trey should decide based on what would make him happiest, but she knew it would be easier for Eugene to accept if it were about the money.

"I wish there was something we could do."

"We just have to let him make his decision," she calmly advised.

The next morning, Trey stepped out of the house with his *Rag* folder and his college books. He started his white, 1973 Chevy Nova and headed past the old boat and onto the highway. Every time he passed the old boat, he endured that moment of pride and guilt. He wondered whether staying to run the business would atone for the mistake he had made. Perhaps that would make things right, erase the blemish, and cleanse his soul.

Trey headed onto the main street in Locksville and pulled into a diagonal parking space in front of the Locksville Publishing building. Locksville Publishing produced a number of local newspapers as well as other publications, including the *River Rat Rag*. He grabbed the folder and entered the building. It was an old building, built in the mid 1800s. The floor creaked as he walked to the counter, and that drew Mrs. Philips from the back room.

"Good morning, Trey. What do you have for me?"

Trey pushed the folder of articles across the counter. "Good morning. These are the articles for the June edition of the *Rag*."

"Well, let's see what we have." She scanned through the articles. She looked at the photos, flipping them over to see the sizing markups Trey had specified. "Looks good. I'll have these typeset today. Do you want to do the layout this afternoon?"

"Yes, I'll be by this afternoon after classes."

"OK, we'll get it set up for you. Lori will be here to help you."

"Sounds good."

"So I hear that you are thinking about a job in Cincinnati."

Trey was annoyed but not surprised that word had traveled so quickly. It was a small town, and any bit of news would set phones to ringing across town. "Well, I have an offer from a company there. I don't know what I'm going to do yet."

"I'd hate to see you go. Your dad really needs you here. The whole town needs you. People think highly of you."

"Thanks, Mrs. Philips. That's nice to hear. There's a lot to think about."

"This is such a nice place. You read the papers and you see all of the riots and murders and hippies. You don't have that here. We've got good people. Sometimes I wish we could just build a wall around the area."

"This is a nice place."

"Sometimes when you grow up in a place like this you don't fully appreciate it because you haven't seen other places. I've lived here all my life and have no desire to leave."

"I might be here forever, too. We'll see. But I'd better be going now. I've got to get to class."

"Have a good day, Trey. We'll get the typesetting done."

Trey headed to Renee's house, pulled into the driveway, and tooted the horn. Renee was Trey's fiancé, and she too would be graduating from the university in June. She was an education major and hoped to teach elementary grades. She skipped down the wooden front porch steps and into the Nova. She set her books at her feet and leaned over to kiss Trey.

Renee used to have long brunette hair, but she had recently cut it to shoulder length. Her mother had advised against it, but she did it anyway. Trey loved it. He thought it made her face look brighter. It made her seem lighter, free from years of keratin history.

"So are we going to school or Cincinnati?" she probed with a smile.

"How do people already know about this? I just got the letter last night."

"Big news travels fast."

Trey shook his head in amazement and backed out of the driveway. They drove along the curvy road that followed the river, then turned south onto the long, straight rural road through farmland.

"They offered me the marketing communication job. Great salary. They want an answer in two weeks."

"What are you going to do?"

"I don't know. The job and the company sound really exciting. I never expected such a great opportunity. It's all the things I like about my job here, and none of the things I don't like. But I don't know if I can leave here, and I don't know if you really want to leave either."

"Trey, I've told you before. I will go wherever you go. I can get a teaching job anywhere they have children."

"IIow about Nome, Alaska?"

"As long as you keep me warm."

They passed farm after farm as they drove through the flat land. Some had old wooden farmhouses; some had both old farmhouses and new houses. Trey knew some of the farmers that lived in this countryside. They were self-reliant, stubbornly independent, and rooted in the land like the crops that were now sprouting. Generation after generation devoted themselves to their families and their businesses, their names prominent in local history books.

"Which way are you leaning?" Renee asked.

Trey shrugged his shoulders. "Right now, I'm leaning toward my coin purse."

After classes, Trey dropped Renee off at her house and headed to the publishing office. He went past the counter into the back room where a row of easels held blank templates for laying out pages for the *Rag*. Mrs. Philips' daughter, Lori, was busy preparing the typeset text for Trey to lay out. The text had been printed in justified columns, and Lori was cutting the text into strips. Then she ran them through the wax machine, which coated the back of the strips so that they would stick to the master template.

"Hey, Trey," Lori called out. "I'll have these for you in a minute."

"Thanks, Lori." Trey knew her well. They went to high school together, and throughout high school, she had dated Les. Lori and Les went to all of the dances — the winter balls, the homecomings, and the proms. Everyone figured they'd marry after high school.

Les worked for his father, Leonard, who owned the gas station in town. It would have been a good start for a marriage except that Les and Leonard grated against each other like chunks of ice during the spring ice flow. Their arguments would drown out the radio playing in the service bay. Just after graduation, when Les turned 18, he packed some bags in the trunk of his Plymouth Duster. He went to Lori's house and begged her to come with him, but she refused to go. He left alone.

"Here you go," she told Trey as she began sticking the strips of typeset text to the shelf above the easels. "Let me know if you need me to rerun anything."

"Thanks very much."

Trey went to work on the layout, cutting the strips to length and pasting them to the master template per his plan. As he worked, the expected question came.

"So are you going to accept the job?" she asked.

"I don't know. It's a tough decision."

"You're lucky to have the opportunity. If I ever get a chance to leave, I'm outta here."

"You had a chance with Les."

"That would have been a disaster. He just got mad and left without a plan. Who knows where he is or what he's doing now."

"Well, this is a nice place and you have a good job working with your mom."

"Yes, it's OK. I just feel trapped here. I wish I could bust down the walls and get out of here."

"What do you really want to do?"

She pondered the question for a moment, then shook her head. "I don't know. I always wanted to live in a city where there's lots to do. I want to see what's out there in the world."

"I've always had that feeling, too," Trey said. "Wanting more but not knowing what. It took me a long time to figure out what I really want."

"You should take that job," Lori advised.

Trey sighed and leaned against the easel. "I wish it were so simple."

The next day after classes, Trey worked the front desk at the office. Rent for summer RV sites was due by the end of May, so there was a steady stream of customers bringing their checks. Knowledge of Trey's job offer was ubiquitous now, so along with the checks came free advice. *You don't want to live in a city. Cities are full of crime. You can't breathe the air. Everything is so expensive in a city. There's no better fishing than what we have right here. Everyone knows everyone here. We take care of each other. You owe it to your family to continue the legacy. Why take a chance? Stick with the tried and true. Be loyal. Appreciate what you've got. You belong here.* The love from the community was overwhelming.

Then Leonard, Les's father and gas station proprietor, walked in. He was a demanding customer, always quick with a complaint. So along with his rental check came some sharp words. "Are you the fella who moved my trailer to the site from storage? It's not level and it's not straight in the site."

"I'm sorry, we can take care of that for you," Trey replied.

"Why couldn't you do it right the first time? I always tell my employees to do things right the first time. There's no excuse for half-assed work."

"We'll get it straightened out."

"Your generation is just too damned lazy. You need to take some pride in your work."

Overhearing the conversation, Eugene emerged from the office and put his hand on Leonard's shoulder. "Let's step outside, Leonard," he said.

Once outside, Eugene grabbed Leonard by the shirt and pushed him against the outside wall of the office. "Now you listen to me. I don't ever want to hear you talking to my boy like that again."

"He did a piss-poor job setting up my trailer."

"First of all, I set up your trailer and I'll come down and make any adjustments you want. But you don't talk to my boy that way. You drove your own boy away and I'll be damned if I'm going to let you drive away mine."

Leonard raised his hands, palms open, and looked down at his feet. The mention of driving Les away hurt more than any punch Eugene could have thrown. "Fine," he mumbled.

Eugene let loose of his shirt. "I'll be down to the site in a few minutes."

Eugene drove the tractor to Leonard's site, backed it up to the tongue, and hitched it up. "What do you want done?" he asked Leonard.

"It needs to be squared up, and I need a leveling board under the back wheels."

Eugene pulled the trailer forward, then backed it up parallel with the site boundary. Leonard put a leveling board under the back wheels, and Eugene pulled it forward onto the board and cut the tractor's engine.

"That's better," Leonard said as he checked the level. "Thank you."

Eugene stood to face Leonard. "Look, I'm sorry I lost my temper. I'm a little sensitive about the possibility of Trey leaving right now."

"I'm sorry, too. I was out of line. You want to pull up a chair and have a beer?"

Eugene had a lot of work to do, but a beer and a chat with Leonard would offer a nice break. "Sure."

Leonard brought out a couple cans of Miller, and they sat in webbed lawn chairs in front of his rig.

"We've known each other a long time," Eugene said. "I really shouldn't have brought up your son. I'm sorry."

"I probably deserved it. It still hurts."

"Have you ever heard from him?"

"No. It'll be four years in June. Left on his 18th birthday. Never heard from him since. I wish I would have done things better, been a better father, not pushed him so hard. You only get one chance to do things right."

"He has your drive, so I'm sure he landed on his feet. It'd be nice if he called you, though."

"Ah, he's bullheaded like me. So what is your son going to do?"

"He hasn't decided yet. Has an offer in Cincinnati, and they offered him a ton of money. Can't compete with that."

"These big companies have the money. They just suck up all of our best kids. What are you going to do if he leaves?"

"I guess I'll do what you're doing. Keep running the business. When I get too old, I'll have to sell it."

"That would be a shame. It's been in your family for more than 50 years."

"I always envisioned him taking it over. Every decision I ever made was based on what would be best for him when he takes over."

"The best laid plans …"

"My dad used to tell me the most important part of selling was creating a compelling vision. But he also told me that even with the most compelling vision, some will walk away."

"You can lead a horse to water …"

Eugene and Leonard finished their beers, then opened two more.

The next morning, Trey and Renee drove to class, through the flatland, past the farms. "How can I walk away?" Trey asked. "Everything is set up for me."

"But do you really want to manage a boat business?" Renee challenged.

"Well, I don't hate the business. There's a lot I like about it. And I owe it to my dad and my grandfather."

"Why do you owe them?"

"Because they built the business for me. And when we have kids, the business will be there for them. It's our family legacy."

"What if they don't want that? What if they want to be teachers or computer programmers?"

Trey sighed. Renee could be so perspicacious. "Everyone that came in yesterday had reasons why I should stay."

"I doubt they thought about it as much as you have. After all, it's your life. You have to write your own script, not follow a script someone else wrote."

"But I don't want to let my family down."

Renee reached over and stroked his thigh as they drove through the countryside. "I know."

After class, Trey dropped Renee off at her house, then went to pick up printed copies of the *Rag*. He dropped off copies to be mailed at the post office, then took copies to each of the local advertisers who agreed to stock the paper in their shops. Then he went home and put a stack of papers on the counter in the office.

Eugene was at the counter and handed him a slip of paper with a phone number. "Someone from Datafoil called you. They want you to call them. It sounded urgent."

Trey went into the back office, closed the door, and dialed the number. When he came back out, Eugene and Ellie were standing together at the counter. Trey was energized. He could have jumped over the counter and performed an end-zone dance, but he suppressed it, knowing how his parents would feel. "Datafoil upped my offer," he said dryly.

"How much?" asked Eugene.

"Ten percent more."

Eugene sighed and nodded as Trey headed for the house. Ellie put an arm around Eugene. They hugged in silence. They both knew the scales had tipped further in favor of Datafoil. There was nothing to be said.

They were embracing when a customer opened the door and stepped up to the counter. "I'm sorry, am I interrupting?" he asked. "I just need a dozen night crawlers."

The Memorial Day weekend arrived, and with it came the crowds. Families sat in front of their RVs chatting, playing cards, and drinking beer. They played Jarts in the grass and rode bikes on the gravel roads. Boaters lined up at the boat launch to slide their vessels into the water. The river was a freeway of joyriders and water skiers.

While customers enjoyed their weekend, Eugene and Trey worked on preparations for Monday's chicken barbecue and dance. They towed the large barbecue into place with the tractor, and they stacked up bags of charcoal. They erected open-sided tents on the pavilion grass to shade the picnic tables, and another open-sided tent over the concrete slab that would become the dance floor. The setup was second nature to them now.

On Monday afternoon, Eugene soaked charcoal in lighter fluid, then piled it in the grill and lit it. When the flame subsided, he spread it to make an even bed of glowing coals in the bottom of the grill. Meanwhile, Trey ran extension cords to the concrete slab and wired the sound system for the band. Ellie and Renee loaded ice chests full of chicken breasts and legs into the trunk of Trey's Nova and drove down to the barbecue area. Soon, the aroma drifted through the RV park and triggered the appetites of all with noses.

As he had done for the last four years, Trey stepped up to the microphone to begin the event. "Ladies and gentlemen," he said, "the River Rats welcome you to the 1979 summer kickoff. We invite you to help yourself to chicken, corn-on-the-cob, salad, beer, and soft drinks. Once again this year, we have music by Locksville's own band, The Four Old Fishermen. So grab some dinner, find a table, and enjoy the music."

Trey placed the microphone in its stand, and the band began to play. He had given the event its initial push, a push big enough to last the evening, perhaps the last push he would ever give it. Or, perhaps, some years down the line, he'd pass the mic to his son or daughter to do the honors. For the moment, though, there was chicken to cook, so he grabbed tongs and joined Renee at the grill.

"Nice speech," she said.

"Were you moved to tears?"

"Only by the smoke," she said, wiping her eyes.

"Will you miss this if we move to Cincinnati?"

"Maybe a little," she replied. Then she whispered into Trey's ear, "I won't miss this band, though."

Trey snorted in agreement. They were old musicians playing old songs to an old audience. They were talented, and some of the songs were good, but Trey's feet yearned for some disco tunes, his ears for some rock and roll.

The food was consumed. The moon rose. The evening was filled with fish stories and laughter, music and the shuffling of feet on the concrete. Trey and Renee stole away to snuggle on the dock and kiss. The only thing they knew for sure was that they would be together for a lifetime. Whether River Rats or city slickers, they would grow together.

Trey reached into his pocket and pulled out his coin purse. It was the one he had since middle school, made of soft plastic and shaped like a football. He squeezed the pointed ends, and it opened like the mouth of a bass. He took out a quarter and returned the coin purse to his pocket.

"Let's do this together," he told Renee. "Heads we go to Cincinnati. Tails we stay here."

Exasperated, Renee sighed. "Flip a coin? Really?"

Trey positioned the quarter on his thumb and held it out. He gave it a flick, and at that moment Eugene called to him, "Hey Trey!" Distracted, he fumbled the coin. It hit the dock and bounced into the water.

Eugene stepped onto the dock. "Trey, could I have a moment with you?"   His words were slurred by an evening of beer.

"Sure," Trey replied.

"I'm going to check on Ellie," Renee said as she excused herself.

"Thanks, Renee," Eugene said, and he sat down next to Trey.

"That Renee sure is a sweet girl," Eugene said to Trey. "You picked a nice one."

"Thanks, Dad."

"You know, son, it was 33 years ago this weekend that I proposed to your mother. I took her out on the *River Rat I* up to Grassy Island. We had a picnic and watched the sun set. That's when I asked her to marry me. She said yes right then and there. We've had a lot of happy years together."

Eugene grew quiet and fidgeted with his hands in his lap. Trey sensed a turmoil within his dad.

"I've been thinking about those days and about something your grandfather said to me before I proposed to her.   I was unsure about asking her to marry me because I didn't know how my folks would feel about it. So I asked him, *Do you think she is the right one for me? How do I know I'm making the right decision?* I ran through all the reasons why I wanted to marry her. We were sitting right over there on the riverbank."

"What did he say?"

"He told me I was analyzing it too much. Worrying about too many things that didn't matter. Worrying too much about what others would think. He told me it's like picking out a favorite star in the night sky. It doesn't matter what someone else might pick. You look and find one that you have a special affinity for."

"And that was Mom?" Trey asked, a little confused.

"Yes. *Always follow your affinities*, he told me. So I got to thinking today that it's not just about marriage. It's about any decision. You get lost if you over-analyze. You paddle up dead-end creeks. You just have to stick to your main channel. Don't worry about what someone else would do or what someone else wants you to do. Do what is right for you. Everything else will fall in place."

Eugene rose and turned to leave. Trey called after him. "Thanks, Dad."

Two golden tassels swayed on the Nova's rear-view mirror as Trey and Renee turned into the River Rats entrance with a U-Haul in tow. It was raining, but newly-degreed Trey and Renee didn't let that dampen their excitement. They stepped out of the car and rushed to the house through the downpour.

Donning his poncho, Trey added his boxes alongside Renee's in the trailer, then shut the trailer door. Trey, Renee, Eugene, and Ellie gathered on the covered porch.

"We're so proud of you," Ellie said as she hugged Trey.

Eugene opened his arms for a hug. "You're making the right move. You're going to do well."

After hugs for Renee, the couple headed through the rain to the Nova.

"Drive carefully!" Ellie shouted to them. "Call us when you get there!"

Ellie and Eugene watched them exit the property and drive away. "I hope everything works out OK for them," Ellie said.

"They'll be fine," Eugene assured her. "Trey's a smart kid, and he's doing what's right for him and Renee. Everything will fall in place."

Trey and Renee headed down the curvy river road, then down the long, straight road past the farms. The sky was dark, sliced occasionally by jagged streaks of lightning. They reached I-75 and merged into the southbound lanes. As they passed through Findlay, the sky began to clear. Rays of sunlight between the scattered clouds shone down on the road ahead.

"Do you think we're doing the right thing?" Trey asked.

"I know we are," Renee assured him.

"I'm going to miss this place."

"Me, too, but it's only a four-hour drive."

"Yeah, but it will be different. We won't be part of it anymore."

"It will always be part of us, though," Renee pointed out.

"Yes. It'll always be in my heart. The town, the river, the campers, the events."

"Everything except The Four Old Fishermen," Renee teased.

"Actually, they'll be in my heart, too."

Renee crinkled her nose. "OK, they can be in your heart, but not in our 8-track."

Paradise Skate

I know why he called it Paradise Skate. It seemed like a good name back then. It promised a blissful refuge, an endless circle of pleasure, and a mesmerizing medley of music and motion. But its neon sign is dark now, its walls scarred with graffiti, and its parking lot paved with broken glass.

Two and a half years ago, though, Paradise Skate was the place for college students to go for roller skating. I was a sophomore at the university then, working on a degree in computer science. It wasn't the major I had intended, but when I took my first programming class I was hooked.

There was a certainty to programming, an ability to encode a series of actions for the computer to perform as directed. If coded correctly, a program would do exactly as it was meant to do, step by step, with no stumbles or falls or rogue actions. That certainty along a path toward a defined goal caught my eye like a distant shimmering light and inspired me to learn more. More languages, more algorithms, more computer systems. I planted myself in the university computer lab and imbibed programming techniques.

In December of 1976, I was in the computer lab making final corrections to a program for one of my classes. I put a few Hollerith cards into the keypunch machine and typed some lines of FORTRAN code. I integrated them into the box of computer cards that held my program. With luck, those changes would allow my program to run correctly, and I would be free to relax over Christmas break.

I gingerly loaded my deck of Hollerith cards into the card reader, being careful not to drop any. Dropping a deck of computer cards would be a catastrophe. Cards had to be in a precise order for the program to work correctly, so having a deck scatter across the floor would require much effort and time to reassemble. If a card glided across the floor and into the realm of lost socks, it would have to be recreated. If a card were to be bent or mutilated, or if it were to pick up a speck of dirt or dust, the program could fail. To avoid this upheaval, I was always meticulous when moving a card deck from my box to the reader.

I pressed the button on the card reader, and they zipped through the reader one-by-one. Then I carefully returned the cards to the box and went out to the hallway to wait for the results. The program would load and run automatically, and its output would be printed by the line printer and placed in my folder by the computer operator.

I sat in the hallway where other students were reviewing their printouts and debugging their syntax and logic errors. As I waited, Jim and Robin came down the hall. They were also sophomores and my roommates in a house we rented off campus. Jim was an engineering major, and, like me, appreciated certainty and precision. Robin was a psychology major drawn to the chaotic mysteries of human behavior.   They had been together through high school and planned to marry after completing college.

"Hey Todd," Jim said, "we're going to Paradise Skate tonight. Want to come?"

"Sure, sounds good."

"Great. We can drive."

I went into the computer lab, picked up the printout, and examined it. Perfection. The program compiled and executed correctly. I was done with schoolwork for the holidays. I went home, changed clothes, and was soon at Paradise Skate with Jim and Robin.

In my size 12 skates, I circled the oval, and with each revolution, the ups and downs of the day faded. Worries about grades were forgotten as I fell into the enchantment of the skating rink. It was a comfortable venue for a single guy. Discos were more intimidating because a guy really couldn't dance alone, but at a skating rink, you didn't need a partner to get on the floor.

They played all of the good music, a little rock and a little disco, everything from the Eagles and Boston to the Bee Gees and Tavares. The music was both energizing and relaxing. I became captive to the music and the gentle buzz of the polyurethane wheels on the smooth wooden floor. I became hypnotized by the disco balls that cast glittering light throughout the room. The space within these four walls was a pleasurable retreat from the pursuits and challenges outside. It felt like paradise.

Owen owned the business, and he loved to stand in his booth at the end of the rink, arranging the music and controlling the lights. His shoulder-length hair and tie-dyed shirts fit him well for his role as disc jockey. He was friendly and approachable, and he made it a point to greet as many of his patrons as possible. He called it Paradise Skate because he wanted to provide a paradise for his patrons, but it was as much a paradise for himself. He was a Vietnam veteran, and this was his escape from miserable memories, a way of coping with the trauma he had endured.

"Please clear the floor," he announced into his microphone.

I skated to the area along the side of the rink and found a seat on a carpeted bench.

"I now welcome to the floor some students from our Saturday class. They call themselves the Skating Angels," Owen announced.

The instructor led a half dozen young skaters onto the floor, the lights dimmed, and the music began. The song was "Heaven Must Be Missing an Angel" by Tavares. The middle-school-aged girls flew gracefully around the oval, following their college-aged instructor. Their bodies bobbed and turned and twisted in time with the music.

They were a well-practiced team of skaters, but my eyes were focused on the instructor.

She wore snug black jeans and a blue knitted sweater. Her body was petite and athletic, and she had short blonde hair styled in a wedge cut. Her moves were smooth and natural, her legs parting and crossing as if she were floating above the floor. She skated backwards as naturally as she skated forward, and her arms and shoulders moved gracefully to maintain her balance.

There was something magical about the way she led her students around the floor, like a mother duck leading a parade of ducklings. They watched her as closely as I watched her, and they mimicked her every move and shift and bodily expression. The aura of her tutelage encompassed all of them. She *was* a skating angel.

Applause filled the rink as the song completed and the featured skaters left the floor. "All skate," Owen announced, and I joined the rush of mediocre skaters onto the floor. Owen would disagree, but it seemed to me a misuse of valuable floor space to allow skaters as undistinguished as myself on the floor when there were those for whom the floor was a canvass awaiting a masterpiece.

I skated to a few songs, then left the floor when Owen announced a couples skate. I passed Jim and Robin as they headed onto the floor, and I crashed on a carpeted bench to wait out the couples skate. I was there for only a minute when I saw the skating angel rolling toward me. She extended her hand to me.

"Would you skate with me?" she asked.

"Well," I stammered, "I'm not a very good skater."

"Skate with me," she insisted.

The depth of her blue eyes and the warmth of her smile enticed me. The fear of embarrassing myself next to such an accomplished skater made me heavy on the bench. My impulse was to resist, but I reached up and took her hand. She led me into the rink and into her world.

"My name is Crystal," she said.

"I'm Todd. I saw you skating earlier. You are very good."

"I saw you watching me. That's why I picked you."

"I'm sure you didn't chose me for my skating skills," I confessed.

"You do fine. You haven't fallen, have you?"

"No, but I can't do the moves you do, like skating backwards."

"Like this?" she asked as she stepped forward and turned to face me, taking both my hands in hers. "It just takes practice."

I tried to keep my feet in synch with hers so as not to trip her, although my attention was consumed by the beauty of her face, the softness of her skin, and the venturesome radiance of her eyes.

"Just look ahead so we don't run into anyone," she advised.

Yes, I best do that, I thought.

"Your class performed very well. You must be a great teacher."

"I don't know about that, but they did good," she replied.

The couples skate ended, and we headed off the floor.

"Thanks for skating with me," she said. Before I could respond, she continued, "Will you skate with me for the rest of the couples skates tonight?"

"Sure!"

We skated to several more couples skates, and after the last skate, as we were changing into our shoes, she turned and asked me, "There's an all-night skate on New Year's Eve. Would you like to meet me here?"

"I would love to," I replied, and my heart skipped.

She gave me a smile and a quick kiss on the cheek. "I'll see you then," she said.

I headed to the car with Jim and Robin. Everything felt different. Usually after skating, my mind was on class assignments and upcoming activities, but on that night, I couldn't think about my studies or plans for visiting my parents. All I could think about was that smile and that kiss and seeing her again on New Year's Eve. I stumbled into the back seat of the car.

As we drove home, Robin turned to me with gossip-hungry ears. "So who is the cute girl you were skating with?"

"Her name is Crystal," I replied. "We're going to the all-night skate on New Years Eve."

"Oooo! Does she go to the university?"

"Yes, she's a freshman."

"What's her major?"

"Physical education. She teaches skating classes part-time."

"Does she live in the dorms?"

"No, she lives with her parents and commutes."

"She's certainly a good skater."

"Much better than me."

"Maybe you'll be spending more time at the skating rink and less time in the computer lab next year!"

The days leading up to New Years Eve passed slowly despite the excitement of the holiday. I wondered how I would keep up with her on the rink, what we would talk about, where this might lead. I wondered whether she would remember our plans and whether she would show up.   I should have gotten her phone number. Nonetheless, when December 31 arrived, I got into my car and drove to the rink.

The walls were decorated with signs welcoming 1977. Balloons were netted to the ceiling awaiting release at the stroke of midnight. Owen was in his booth orchestrating the music and the lights, pointing and waving at the skaters he knew as they passed the booth. I gave him a quick wave and he pointed at me.

As I skated, I scanned the floor and the bench area looking for Crystal. So many unfamiliar faces were coming through the doors, gathering at the skate rental desk, and changing from shoes to skates at the benches. Then I felt someone grab my waist from behind and heard that voice. "Looking for me?" she asked with that confident demeanor.

"There you are," I said, and she spun around in front of me, skating backward.

"I'm glad you came. I was worried that you wouldn't," she admitted.

"I was worried, too. I've been thinking about you every day."

Like celestial bodies in a solar system, we revolved around the oval in the radiance of the disco balls and the groove of the music. With each revolution, we learned a little more about each other as we unwound the stories of our young lives. She was wearing blue jeans and a black T-shirt with a picture of Rod Stewart and the words "Tonight's the Night."

"He's my lover," she said with more adulation that any fan should have. "I'm going to request his song." She pulled us to a stop below Owen's control booth.

"Can you play this?" she asked with two hands pointing at her shirt and, at the same time, the small, firm breasts it clothed.

"Nice," he replied with a wink. "Will do."

He set the record on one of the turntables and cued the song. As the intro played, he announced, "Whatever you're looking forward to — a new year, a new dream, a new love — tonight's the night!"

Crystal and I skated side-by-side, and I felt hopeful about things to come and things that Crystal and I might share in the new year. When midnight came and the skaters gathered on the floor, I held her hand. We joined in the countdown. As the balloons rained down upon us, I pulled her hips close to me, she put her arms around my neck, and we shared a long, deep new year's kiss. Her blue eyes and dauntless smile suggested 1977 could be a good year.

We skated a few more rounds, then she led me off the floor. "Let's go sit in the employee lounge," she said. "I need a cigarette."

I followed her though a door near the skate rental desk, then behind the racks of roller skates, to a small room with a refrigerator, tables, chairs, and bean bag chairs. We pushed two bean bag chairs together and plopped ourselves down. She pulled a pack of Winston cigarettes and a lighter from her pocket.

"I didn't know you smoked," I said. I had never smoked or had any close friends that smoked. In high school, there were groups of stoners that hung out on the corner before and after school smoking, but they were in a different world than me.

"I do. You don't?"

"No," I replied meekly, not wanting to draw attention to any difference between her and me.

"Does it bother you?"

"No, not really," I lied, thinking about the smoke spoiling the tissues of her tiny lungs. "I'm just surprised because you are so athletic."

She exhaled a puff of smoke, leaned toward me, and gave me a kiss. "I can handle it."

She seemed like someone who could handle anything, but I wondered if I could handle her smoking. My nose itched. My sweater soaked up the smell. My eyes watered, yet they could not wander from the tender beauty of her face. A little smoke could not obscure that radiance.

Throughout the night we alternated between skating, crashing on the bean bags, drinking pops, and kissing. We exchanged phone numbers and addresses and made plans to go out again the next weekend. As the sun rose on New Year's morning, we embraced in the parking lot, spoke of how much we'd miss each other during the week, and headed for our homes.

It was hard to wait a whole week to see her again, so I called her a few times during the week. Sometimes her dad answered.   Rather than the customary *Hello,* he would pick up the phone, stay silent for awhile, then gruffly say *Yeah?* I would ask if Crystal was home, and he would set down the phone without any reply, then in a few minutes she would pick up. He was intimidating, and I grew nervous about meeting him.

As I drove to her house that Saturday evening, I hoped that his disposition was just poor telephone etiquette. I turned my Pinto onto the road she lived on and scanned the address numbers on mailboxes. It was a rural area not far from the university with large lots and unkempt houses. I found her house. Its driveway was covered with snow except for the tracks of a rusted, bronze Dodge Monaco that sat in front.   I turned and followed the tracks so as not to get stuck in the snow.

The rollup door on the attached garage was severely dented as if a car had rammed it. The paint on the wooden structure was faded. The two small windows in front were covered not with curtains, but with sheets. I trudged through the snow to the small, railing-less stoop and stomped the snow off my feet. There was no doorbell, so I knocked on the aluminum screen door.

The interior door opened and in front of me was Crystal's dad. He wore a stained T-shirt and baggy grey work pants. His face was stubbled with whiskers, his hair uncombed. He had a slice of yellow cheese hanging from his mouth. "Yeah?" he greeted me.

"I'm Todd," I said nervously, "here to pick up Crystal."

He chewed on his cheese as he contemplated me. Then he shut the interior door, forcing a powerful whiff of alcohol through the torn screen.

A few moments later, Crystal opened the door and invited me in. She introduced me to her mother who was sitting in the corner watching TV. The phone on the table under the living room window rang.

Her dad stumbled to the phone, picked up the handset, and remained silent. Then he hung up, pulled out the wire, and hurled the phone across the living room into the kitchen. He stuffed another slice of cheese into his mouth and washed it down with beer.

"We're going," Crystal said, and she led us out the door. I didn't know what to think. It wasn't the polite interrogation one expects when meeting a date's parents for the first time. They barely acknowledged me. They asked no questions. There was no need or opportunity to reassure them that I would take care of their daughter and have her back at a reasonable hour.

We drove to the pizza parlor and ordered pizza and pop.

"I don't think your dad likes me," I said to Crystal.

"He likes you OK," she replied.

"How can you tell?"

"He didn't hit you."

I wondered if he had hit any of her past dates. I wondered if I was in a probationary period and could be hit in the future if he took a disliking to me. I wondered if he had ever hit her.

"What was the deal with the phone?"

"He's probably late paying a bill. If he doesn't want to talk to someone, he chucks the phone."

"I think he had too much to drink tonight."

"About usual for his day off. On work days, he goes to the bar after work. He takes me with him sometimes."

"Do they let you in?"

"Yeah, he knows the owner. He orders drinks for me. Maybe you can come with us some time. It's cool."

"Maybe." I didn't want to tell her that I didn't drink much alcohol. All I ever had was low-alcohol beer at a disco near the university, and I didn't care much for it. I preferred to be sober and in control.

"You don't drink, do you?" she surmised.

"Not much." She was certainly astute. I stared at the pop in front of me.

"It's cool." She leaned toward me, lowered her head so her blue eyes could catch mine. "I like that you're different. Tell me more about you."

I told her a little about my high school activities and the sports I played. I told about discovering computer science in my first year of college, and how I knew right away that programming is what I wanted to do as a career.

"I don't know anything about computers," she said.

"When did you know that you wanted to be a physical education teacher?"

She hesitated, subtly shrugging her shoulders. "I liked playing sports in high school. I did cross-country and track. They called me Featherweight. That's why I have this tattoo."

She turned around and showed me the tattoo on the back of her neck. It was two, grey feathers inked horizontally as if they were floating in the wind. I never liked tattoos. They seemed like blemishes on an otherwise perfect work of art. On Crystal, though, they seemed natural, complementing her lightness. Like feathers from a tiny bird struggling to fly in the wind.

"Cool," I said. "It looks nice on you."

"I'm not sure I want to be a PE teacher, though. There's a lot of anatomy and health stuff you have to take."

"You did a great job teaching the Skating Angels."

"It was OK, but I get tired of it. Too much work."

"You'll do fine," I encouraged.

Her eyes were focused downward at the pizza. "Todd, I should tell you something. I know I told you I was in college, but I'm not in college anymore. I dropped out."

"Really? What happened?"

"I flunked some of my classes last quarter. I just got tired of it and decided to drop out."

"Are you going to go back later?"

"No. I'm just not into it."

"What did your parents say?"

She shrugged her shoulders. "They didn't care. They thought college was a waste of time anyway."

I had heard so many lectures about the importance of education and the importance of being disciplined in pursuit of goals. I figured it to be a universal lesson that all parents taught. Having met her dad, the mirror she looked into to see who she was, I could see that wasn't true.

"Do you hate me now?" she asked.

Those blue eyes. Those enticing lips. That slim, athletic body that could float so gracefully and confidently over the skating floor. She seemed to accept and even like the differences she saw in me. Now she waited to find out if I could accept the differences I saw in her.

She had lied to me, but it was a smallish lie. And she smoked and she drank, but she was still an angel. Maybe she would change.

I took her hand, and squeezed it tightly. Her eyes met mine and I simply said, "It's cool."

January turned to February, but our daily phone talks and weekends together kept us warm that winter. She was curious about my programming study, so I invited her to see the computer lab and to listen to records at my house.

We stomped the snow off of our shoes before we entered the Computer Science Building. It was a Saturday, so there were only a few students working in the lab. We stood in the keypunch area looking through the window into the room that housed the computer. On a table in the center of the room was the computer, an IBM 360 mainframe, and next to it was the line printer spewing pages of green and white computer paper.

"Check it out," she said. "I've never seen a computer before."

I explained the functions of the system components, including the tape drives, the disk drives, and the operator console.

"Let me show you something," I said as I took out a small deck of cards from my coat pocket. "These are Hollerith cards. See, they have patterns of holes for each character typed at the top of the card. The cards are read by that card reader over there." I took her to the card reader, inserted my card deck, and pressed the button. "This is a little program I wrote for you. The computer will run the program, and we'll get the printout in a little while."

While we waited, we strolled around the room looking at the keypunch machines. She tapped awkwardly on a keyboard. I could see interest and curiosity on her face. Perhaps there was something I could do to amplify that interest. Perhaps I could encourage her to get back in college.   Perhaps all that was required was a little debugging.

The operator emerged and began dropping printouts in the rack of folders, and I fetched the printout from my program. I led her out of the lab and handed it to her.

"Happy Valentine's Day," I said.   She opened the listing to see a heart printed with asterisks on the page. Within the heart were our names, Todd & Crystal.

"I'm taking a computer graphics class," I explained.

"Check it out!" she said. She swung her arms over my shoulders and gave me a kiss. "I love you, Todd."

"I love you, too," I replied.

We drove off-campus to my house, chatted with Jim and Robin, then retreated to my room to listen to music. I set the stack of Hollerith cards on the nightstand, and she explored my collection of LP records. One by one, she handed me albums she wanted to hear, and I added them to the record changer. We laid together on the bed to listen to the music.

"You are so different," she said.

"How so?"

"Most guys just want one thing."

I contemplated that for a moment, then replied. "I want just one thing, too. You."

She cuddled closer to me, laying her head on my chest. As each album side completed, the record changer dropped a new album, and the needle found the beginning of the groove.

"Is it OK if I smoke?" Crystal asked.

I nodded.

She sat up and pulled a cigarette from her pocket, but it was not a Winston. "OK if I smoke a joint?" she clarified.

"I guess. I didn't know you smoked that."

"I like a buzz while listening to music. It's relaxing."

She found an empty pop can in the wastebasket to use as a receptacle for her ashes. She lit the joint, took a drag, and offered it to me. I declined. A lemony smell of burning leaves filled the room and blended with the music. With each song, with each breath of hazy air, my mind grew heavy and at peace. I felt the vibrations of "More Than a Feeling" by Boston as I watched Crystal breathe in and breathe out, her small breasts rising and falling, her lips gently caressing the joint.

Side 1 of the Boston album completed, and the next album dropped. It was the Eagles. "Hotel California." Like the smoke in the room, those lyrics penetrated me. I could see my dream of a programming career, a shimmering light far in the distance. So much closer was Crystal, lying in the bed next to me, finishing her joint, and turning to me with that smile and those eyes.

She was so imperfect, so mismatched, yet her smile outshone that light. Immersed in the dizzying smoke, we kissed. We touched. Light as a feather, she rolled atop me, her lips on mine, her breasts against my chest. I slipped my hands under her top. I pushed it up and over her head, then cast it aside where it landed on the nightstand, scattering the Hollerith cards across the floor.

February melted into March, and most of the snow was gone from her driveway as I pulled in to pick her up. She said she didn't feel like skating that day. Her dad was at work, and her mother was away.

"Let's just listen to some jams," she suggested, leading me to her room.

It was a small room, fitting just her twin bed and a small dresser. On the dresser was a framed photo of a girl. She looked to be about Crystal's age. She was wearing a bikini, standing in front of a Corvette, and holding a margarita.

Crystal loaded some records on the changer, then opened a dresser drawer and pulled out a joint and a lighter.

"Would you smoke with me?" she asked in the same enticing way that she asked that first question in December, *Would you skate with me?*

Her blue eyes locked onto mine, inviting me, tempting me. This tiny room, closed off from the rest of the world, could be paradise, with all the pleasures of her touch and the buzz of a joint. She took my hand, and we sat on the edge of the bed. She lit the joint, took a drag, and exhaled the white smoke into the room. She handed me the joint.

"Smoke with me," she encouraged. *Skate with me,* I recalled.

I so wanted to skate with her and to smoke with her and to spend every moment with her, but I smiled and shook my head ever so slightly.

"It's cool," she said.

"Who is the girl in the picture?" I asked.

"That's my best friend, Annie. We work together."

"Does she teach skating, too?"

"We're partners."

"Like in a business?"

"Kinda," she said. She took a long drag from her joint, released the smoke, then turned to me. "Will you be cool with it if I tell you?"

"Yes," I said without any idea what I was supposed to be cool about.

"Annie and I work together selling marijuana. Columbia Gold mostly. And sometimes cocaine and other stuff."

I felt as if I had been broadsided by another skater on the rink. I felt as if her words had interrupted the harmony of circling skaters and had caused a chain-reaction pileup with me on the bottom.

"Is this, like, selling to your friends?" I asked hopefully.

"No, we sell to smaller dealers in the area."

"Do you make a lot of money doing this?"

"Yeah. It pays a lot more than teaching. Annie and I bought that Corvette together for cash," she said proudly, pointing to the picture.

"What if you get caught?"

"I can handle it."

I did my best to remain cool on the outside, but inside, I was in turmoil trying to reconcile the conflicting images passing through my mind. An athletic girl running track with a cigarette between her lips. A graceful skater doing a spin with a joint in her hand. A teacher leading her young students to a back-alley drug dealer.

"Why do you do it?"

"It's just something I'm into."

"Do your parents know?"

"No. If they knew, they'd want a cut of the money."

"Is this something you're doing just for now? Just to make some money? What about your future? What about your career? What about your talents? What do you want to do with your life?"

She shrugged and finished her joint, then laid back on the bed. I laid on my side next to her, and she pulled my face close to hers. We kissed. We pulled our bodies close. I ran my hand over the feathers on her neck, down her solid back, and to her petite but muscular legs. Only kisses came from her tender lips, no answers. My questions scattered like a deck of computer cards across the floor.

Led Zeppelin was playing. "Stairway to Heaven."

It made me wonder about the paths we were on, two different paths intersecting in this time and place. I wanted to reach out and pull her to my path. She could teach; I could program. But she was pulling me to her path, too. *Would you skate with me? Skate with me.*

The next morning, I sat at the breakfast table with Robin. Jim had already left for class. I silently sipped my coffee and spooned my cereal, and Robin sensed the turmoil spinning in my head.

"What's wrong, Todd?" she asked.

I didn't try to deny my uneasiness. Robin was too good at seeing through things. She had a knack for getting at the crux of personal issues.

"Everything is falling apart," I replied.

"Like what?"

"My grades for one. I just can't concentrate on school anymore. All I can think about is Crystal."

She nodded. "You love her."

"We love each other, but I found out some things about her."

"What?"

"She's turning out to be way different than I thought." I took a breath and tried to organize my thoughts. "She smokes, she drinks, she smokes pot, she dropped out of college. Yesterday I found out she's a drug dealer."

I could see the shock on Robin's face. She silently stared at her coffee cup for a few minutes. For someone who was always quick with words, her silence amplified the seriousness of my situation.

"She is so different," I added.

"I'll say. Much different."

"I don't know how to help her."

"You can't fix her," Robin said. "She's not a program you can debug."

"But I want to help her."

Robin's eyes narrowed and she bit her lip. Shaking her head, she said, "Unless she wants to change, there's nothing you can do. You can't make her into what you want her to be."

I didn't want to hear her say that. I wanted to engineer a fix that would pull Crystal from her road to mine. Still, I knew she was right.

April brought rain that turned the remaining snow to slush. It was neither winter nor spring, but some uncomfortably undefined in-between state, much like Crystal and me. She still smoked cigarettes and weed, drank in the bar with her dad, and sold drugs. We still said *I love you* to each other. We still went to movies and pizza parlors and listened to albums in our rooms. And we still skated in the blissful refuge of Paradise Skate, round and round the circle of pleasure, self-sentenced prisoners of the present.

When I picked her up to go skating that Saturday, I had no idea that all would change that night. I sloshed my way to her stoop and knocked on the door. When Crystal opened the door, I could see her mother asleep in front of the television and her dad asleep in his chair, his hand frozen around a beer can. It was all as usual. We walked out to my Pinto and drove to Paradise Skate.

We skated to song after song, weaving around other skaters, moving with the beat of the music. Crystal was exceptionally radiant that night, her eyes reflecting the disco lights, her smile illuminating the room. Her hand felt a part of mine as we circled.

In a special session, Crystal and the Skating Angels performed a roller dance in the center of the rink. They did step overs and shifts and spins. Crystal had such balance, such leg strength, such beauty and talent. I wondered whether her parents had ever seen her skate. Or teach.

At the end of the night, we changed into our shoes, and Crystal said, "I need to help Owen with something. Do you mind waiting for me? It'll only be a half hour."

"No problem," I replied. "Anything I can help with?"

"No. Just wait in the car."

So I flowed out to the parking lot with the crowd and watched as the parking lot emptied. I tuned my FM converter to my favorite station, reclined my seat, and relaxed. I had homework to do that weekend, including some reading and some programming, but I didn't want to think about it now. I just wanted to think about that angel.

Soon after the parking lot emptied, a white panel van crept into the lot and stopped by the front door. A driver and a passenger got out of the van, and it was the driver that caught my eye. As he exited, he picked up something from under the seat and slid it under his belt. The men walked around to the back. They loaded some cartons onto a hand truck and wheeled them to the front door. Owen and Crystal greeted them and took possession of the boxes.

Through the glass entrance doors, I watched Owen open the boxes and inspect them one by one, then hand an envelope to one of the men. He shook hands with each of them, then Crystal stepped outside and gave each man a hug. The men returned the hand truck to the van and shut the doors. The driver removed the object from his belt and put it under the driver seat. I could see that it was a gun. They drove away.

Awhile later, Owen and Crystal exited the building, locked the doors, and hugged. Owen headed to his car, and Crystal headed to mine.

"All done," she said.

"What was that all about?" I asked.

"Just a delivery," she replied.

"The delivery guy had a gun."

"It's no big deal," she dismissed.

"So what were they delivering? Skates?"

"No," Crystal chuckled. "I think you know."

"Tell me."

"I need you to be cool with it."

"I am cool."

"It was a shipment of weed and angel dust."

"Why is it being shipped here?"

"Because Owen makes dime bags and sells them here."

I processed that for a moment. What had seemed so distant, almost theoretical, was real now. What had seemed like paradise was a back alley. What had seemed like an angel had crumbled to dust.

"It's not a big deal. Are you cool with it?" she asked.

I shook my head. "I don't know. I don't like it."

She drew a breath. "I love you, Todd. I want you to be cool with it."

I started the car, and we drove through the darkness in silence. We pulled into her driveway. I shut off the engine and turned to her. "Crystal, I'm not cool with it. With you being a drug dealer."

"You don't have to be involved, Todd. I don't want you to be involved. I shouldn't have helped Owen tonight."

"It's not just about tonight. I don't want to be involved with a drug dealer. I want you to quit."

I took her hand. I held it tight. It felt so natural in mine, but it was not natural at all.

"Can you handle it? Please?"

It was a yes or no question, and I so wanted to say yes. It would have been easier in the short term, but would have prolonged the slushy uncertainty. It took all of the strength I could muster to suppress my trembling irresolution and say that simple word. "No."

I let go of her hand. There were tears on her face as she turned away, opened the car door, and sloshed to the front porch.

For days, I hoped the phone would ring. I hoped to hear her voice telling me she was quitting the drug business. That she was giving up cigarettes and weed. That she was going back to college to pursue a career as a PE teacher. The phone never rang.

One May evening, Jim, Robin, and I were watching the local TV news. With a picture of Owen in the upper corner of the screen, the anchorman reported that Paradise Skate was being closed because of drug trafficking. Nothing was said about Crystal, and although I was curious, I had homework to do. I had a programming project to complete. I had finals to study for.

I felt the reassuring hand of Jim on my shoulder, and Robin sat next to me and took my hand in hers. Their friendship helped me get through that evening and the next two years. It helped me re-focus on my computer classes. It helped me reassemble my deck of Hollerith cards and keep them in order. It helped me earn my diploma and a job offer in California.

Jim volunteered to drive me to the airport when I left for my new job, and we stopped by the boarded-up Paradise Skate on our way. It was no longer a blissful refuge or endless circle of pleasure or mesmerizing medley of music and motion. It was no longer a paradise, and perhaps it never could have been. Paradise is not a walled retreat, but an opened-ended adventure. It is not a pleasurable escape, but a sometimes heart-wrenching commitment. True paradise is not a place; it is a pursuit.

At the airport, I said good-bye to Jim and boarded the airplane. It was a night flight, and I looked down at islands of light as I flew across the country. I listened to music with my headphones. "More Than a Feeling" played, and I thought about that February day with Crystal in my room. I thought about all she could have been, but she was always slipping away along a different path.

I looked out into the darkness, wondering if she was down there, maybe stumbling, maybe skating. Then we passed into California, and the cabin crew prepared for arrival. As we made our nighttime descent, I could see the blackness below, then, suddenly, the brilliant, shimmering light of Silicon Valley.

The Blizzard of '78

I had only one goal that January morning: pick up data files from three clients and get them to the office for data entry and processing.

My wife, Emily, and I owned a computer services business in northwest Ohio. We started it while we were in college. Emily was a computer science major and programming whiz. I was a business major. With some help from professors, we leased an IBM 360 system and office space near the university. We had COBOL and RPG applications for billing, payroll, inventory management, and subscriptions, and Emily customized applications for some of our clients.

Business fell on us like snow, like a blizzard really, and we were limited only by how fast we could shovel it. Businesses throughout the region were thirsty for ways to streamline their information processing without having to learn about and invest in computers, so requests for our services piled up.

It was a good problem to have, at least that's what we told ourselves. It required long hours and seven-day workweeks. Vacations were out of the question. Even our honeymoon had to be abbreviated to a weekend at Marblehead on Lake Erie. A relentless focus on one mission was the key to success. If we could stay disciplined on each task and each goal, we could accomplish something great. We could bring the power of computing to our region's businesses.

Dad had always encouraged me to think big and be disciplined. His Depression-abbreviated education had limited his opportunities, but he was a disciplined worker. His job as a factory maintenance mechanic had provided our family with a comfortable life. It had provided me with a college education and the chance to achieve bigger goals. He was proud.

Before heading out on that January morning, I primed myself with bits of information to use during the obligatory small talk. That included some facts about the Dallas Cowboys' victory over the Denver Broncos in the Super Bowl. I was never a football fan; chatter about the trivia of a game seemed like an incredible waste of energy to me. Nonetheless, customers liked to talk about stuff like that, so knowing a little was important to customer relations.

Small talk would have to be minimized that morning, though. They were predicting heavy snow, so I needed to pick up the data files and get back to the office before the weather got bad.

Emily had already left for the office, so I locked up as I headed out of our rented apartment and headed to my Trans Am. I drove north for ten miles across the flat farmland. Large, wet snowflakes were already falling, so I stretched the speed limit as much as I could in order to complete my rounds before the storm. I drove over the bridge to the next town and parked at the Town Hall. My first visit was with Mrs. Johnson of the town's water utility.

"Good morning," I greeted as I stepped up to the counter. "Have you got some data files for me?"

"Good morning, Robert." She was elderly, and she spoke as slowly as she walked.

Seeing a document box on the counter, I asked, "Are these the files?"

Halfway from her desk to the counter, she replied, "Yes, but I need to show you some things."

She progressed at her own pace, and when she finally arrived at the counter, she took out a bound customer report that we had generated for her. Some of the pages had dog-eared corners. She licked a finger and turned to the first marked page.

"We have some corrections we need to make. It's important that we get everything right," she began. "Now this first one is a misspelling. Mrs. Peterson's name is spelled with an "o,"not an "e." She is of Swedish descent, and in Sweden, "Peterson" is spelled with an "o." Danish Petersons who immigrated to English-speaking countries also tend to spell their names with an "o" in keeping with English conventions."

"OK, Mrs. Johnson," I interrupted. "Are all of your corrections marked on these pages?"

"Yes. Now this next one is an error in the mailing address. It should be 830, not 850."

"If these are all marked, we can make the corrections. We don't need to go through all of them."

"It's important that we get this right. I want to make sure you understand all of the changes."

"Mrs. Johnson, it looks like you did a thorough job marking the corrections. We don't need to go through them all here. If we have questions, we can call you." She was on a different speed setting than me, and my heart rate increased as I felt the urgency to collect the files and get to the next client.

"I'm happy to go through them with you."

"Thanks, but that's not necessary. I do need to get going so I can get back before the weather gets bad."

"I understand. They say it could be as bad as last year."

"I hope not. We'll get the corrections made. And if we have any questions, we'll call you."

"Very well then. Thank you, Robert."

"Thank you, Mrs. Johnson."

I put the bound copy back into the box, grabbed the box, and hurried toward the door. The snow was coming down faster, and I could not afford to waste any more time.

My next stop was the grocery store. I found the owner, Mr. Jensen, in his office.

"How about those Cowboys!" he said as I entered.

"It was a great game," I replied.

"And how about that Staubach!"

"He was good," I replied. In my worry about getting back on the road, I drew a blank on the facts I had studied, and I forgot who Staubach was. Trying to move things along, I said, "So you have payroll information for me?"

"Good, hell! He was great! Seventeen pass completions to Morton's four."

I thought about the college students who would be showing up in the evening to help us with the data entry. We would need to get these files organized so they could get that work done as quickly and accurately as possible.

"The first Super Bowl in the Superdome could not have turned out better," he said, handing me the box of timecards. "Here you go, Robert."

"Thanks, we'll get on this."

I hurried out the door, put the box in the back seat with Mrs. Johnson's box. One more to go. I drove over to see Mr. Moser, owner of the sporting good store. We did sales reports for him. He was a friendly guy. I liked him, but he loved to talk. This one would be a challenge.

"Robert!" he called out as I entered the old building.

"Hey Mr. Moser. I don't have long. I have to get back before the storm. I just want to pick up the sales data."

"Here you go," he replied, pushing a box of sales receipts across the counter to me. I thought I was home free. I thought I could say thanks and leave, but he continued. "Let me show you the new doll flies I just got in."

He led me to the fishing tackle aisle and took one off the display. "These are going to fly off the shelf when the Walleyes come up the river this spring. Guys are going to catch a lot of fish with these lures. Look at the detail in the head."

To me it was a ball of lead with a hook and some colorful feathers tied to it. I had no idea why a fish would be attracted to it, but he was going to tell me.

"Just look how nicely the head is painted. Sparkly pastel colors. And look at the eyes. That's the key. That's what attracts the Walleye. These are very high quality."

I nodded in agreement, of course. "Very nice."

"Hey, do you and Emily enjoy tobogganing? I just got a couple of toboggans in. Take a look." He led me to a display of glossy, wooden toboggans.

"We don't really go sledding. The business consumes all of our time."

"Take it from another business owner. You gotta make time for yourselves. Get out and do things."

"Someday, maybe. Right now, we have to stay focused on the business."

"We're getting some snow. You could get a toboggan and go over to the big hill this weekend and relieve a little stress. And when's the first baby going to come along? You'll have the toboggan and you can pull the little one around in the yard in the wintertime. Babies love toboggan rides."

"It's going to be a long time before we have a baby, not to mention a yard. But speaking of snow, I've got to get going before the roads get bad."

"OK, Robert. You take care. And don't let business snow you in."

"We'll get the data entry done and generate your reports."

With my rounds done, I headed back to the car. It was noon already. The snow was coming down thick, and now the wind was blowing hard. I scraped the icy snow off the windshield, then headed over the bridge and south toward the office. The windshield iced up faster than the wipers could clear it. I had to stop a few times to clear it with my scraper.

When I turned onto Dix Road I stopped one more time to scrape the windshield. Dix Road was a narrow two-lane county road with ditches on both sides. It was all farmland and an occasional farmhouse and barn. I had taken this road often, but the driven snow obscured everything that was familiar. The flatlands had few obstacles to impede the winds. With a clear windshield, wipers running at full speed, and the determination of a fledgling entrepreneur, I proceeded intently down the snow-covered road.

Tire ruts from another vehicle were faintly visible, so I tried to stay in those ruts to keep from getting stuck. I could only hope the driver who made those ruts hadn't run off the road. The intensity of the wind was like I had never seen before, and soon those tire ruts were completely filled with snow. I now had only telephone poles and an occasional mailbox to suggest the location of the pavement, and even those were just shadows in a veil of white.

Everything was white, and I could barely see beyond the end of the hood, but I knew I had to maintain my forward momentum. If I slowed, I would get stuck in the rapidly accumulating snow. I blocked everything else from my mind, kept my foot on the accelerator, and held the steering wheel steady, driving more by feel than by sight.

Then I felt a heavy drag on the right front tire. I felt the rear of the car swing around to my left. I felt the nose of the car sink deep into the snow-filled ditch on the right. The engine stalled, and the only sound was the howling wind.

I put the car in park and restarted the engine. It started right up, so I put it in reverse and gave it a little power. The wheels spun. I tried rocking it, shifting the car into drive then reverse, hoping that I could back it out of the ditch, but I could gain no traction.

"Come on, God. Give me a break!" I pleaded.

I was not going to give up. The business depended on me getting these files to the office, and no snowstorm was going to stand in my way.

I reached to the passenger side and grabbed the floor mat, then I forced open my door, pushing it against a wall of snow. I grabbed the driver side door mat and stepped outside into the waist-deep snow. I threw the door mats toward the rear of the car and trudged up and out of the snow-filled ditch.

The rear wheels were completely buried, so I used my hands to dig the snow away. I should have carried a shovel in the trunk, but I had overlooked that detail. I should have carried a bag of sand in the trunk, but I had overlooked that detail, too. My mind had been on bigger issues. This solution would work, though. It had to work. Failure was not an option.

When I had snow cleared from around the wheel, I slid the floor mat behind it, then I did the same for the passenger side rear wheel. These would provide the traction I needed to get back on the road.

I descended back to the driver-side door and got into the car. I rubbed my hands together to restore warmth, then shifted the car into reverse. I gently applied power, visualizing the traction those floor mats would provide, envisioning the car climbing out of the ditch's grip, but the wheels spun. The car did not move.

"Dammit!" I hollered as I banged on the steering wheel. A few louder curses were no competition for the howling wind outside. Just a few moments ago I had control. I was making progress. I was on my way. Now I was stuck.

I shut off the engine and sat back, watching the ruthless wind deposit more snow on the hood of the car. Inch by inch the snow climbed up the windshield. Soon the entire car would be buried. I resigned myself to the only option I had, finding a house and calling for help.

I penciled out options in my mind. I could call a tow truck to pull me out of the ditch. I could call Emily to have her pick up the files and me, but could either of them even reach me now? Everything was out of balance. Everything was in chaos.

I pulled my coat hood over my head, opened the door, and stepped into the blowing white. I wanted to reach into the back seat to grab the data files in case I could find a way to get them to the office, but with the intensity of the storm, there was no way to keep the boxes dry. The wind would blow off the lids; the snow would soak the papers. I shut and locked the door and hoped the files would remain dry and safe.

I climbed out of the ditch and to the road. Back in the direction I had come, I could make out a faint shadow, a house-shaped area of grey in the whiteness. I trudged in that direction. In some places the snow was only six inches deep; in other places it had drifted to five or six feet.

I reached the house, an old three-story farmhouse, and I climbed the steps to the front porch. The porch floor was uneven; what paint was left on the siding was peeling. I feared that it was vacant and that I'd have to go farther down the road to another house, but how far would that be? Or perhaps I could break in and take shelter here. I knocked on the door. Once, and then again, louder.

A young woman about my age opened the door, and I breathed a sigh of relief.

"Hi, I got stuck in a ditch down the road." I explained, "Could I borrow your phone to call for help?"

The woman looked closely at me. "Robert?"

"Susie?" I replied. *Oh God*, I thought. It was frustrating enough to be stuck in a ditch and have to call for help, but having to ask Susie for help was humiliating.

"Come in," she invited. "The electricity just went out. You can try the phone." She pointed to the phone on table in the living room.

I stomped my feet on the porch, and wiped them on the mat. I walked across the oval braided rug on the living room floor to the telephone. I picked up the receiver and listened for a dial tone, but there was none. I hammered repeatedly on the plunger in the handset rest, but the phone was dead. I cursed under my breath as I replaced the receiver. "The phone is out."

"It's not surprising. This storm is pretty bad," Susie said.

"I'm trying urgently to get some important files back to the office. Do you think you could drive me or let me borrow your car?"

"Sorry, I don't drive in weather like this, and my little Gremlin would get blown away by this wind. You never liked it anyway," she replied.

I had forgotten that she drove a 1970 Gremlin. "Yeah, you're right," I admitted. "Do you think any of your neighbors have a four-wheel drive vehicle?"

"I don't know. The nearest neighbor is a mile down the road, and they're in their eighties. You might as well take your coat off and sit down. You aren't going to get anywhere in this storm. The radio says it's going to be bad."

I sighed in frustration. "I suppose you're right. Hopefully, the phones will be fixed soon so I can call for help."

Susie's face and her voice were familiar, but her body was a little fuller. As I sat down, I realized she was expecting.

"I didn't know you lived out here," I said. It had been more than four years since I had seen her. We went to high school together, to a winter dance together, and to concerts and plays. She was pretty. We had held hands and kissed, and we had fought and argued. When we broke up, she started going with Billy of all people.

"Me and Billy have been renting this house for about six months. He works for the county now."

"So you two are still together?"

"We got married after high school. We lived with my mom and dad for a few years. I got a job at the *County Weekly* doing subscriptions and billing. Billy got a job at the county maintenance department. He got called in this morning to drive snowplow."

Maintenance, I thought. She could have married a guy with grander goals. Her looks and her brains gave her plenty of choices, but she opted for Billy. Maybe it was a good match for her since she never seemed to have grand goals herself.

"And we're starting a family." She smiled and gave her tummy a pat.

"That's great. Is it your first?"

"Yes. If it's a boy it will be Billy Jr. If it's a girl it will be Molly."

"I bet your mom and dad are excited, too."

"They moved out west. I don't hear much from them. Would you like a pop?" I nodded and she went to the kitchen and returned with a bottle of Hoffman's pop. "Lemon is the only flavor I have."

"Thank you." I twisted off the metal screw-top and took a swig.

"What have you been doing since high school?" she asked.

"Well, I went to college and got a business degree. I met Emily in college, and we got married. She's a computer science major. And we run a computer services business doing data processing for local businesses."

"You were always gung-ho," she replied. "I don't want nothing to do with computers. My boss is talking about going to computers at the newspaper, but I hope he doesn't. We have it under control the way we're doing it now."

I should have bitten my tongue, of course, but she would find out eventually. "You are going to computers."

"What?"

"My company is going to be computerizing subscriptions, billing, and ads for the *County Weekly*."

I could tell she wanted to curse, but she wasn't that type. She was not above raising a middle finger to me, though.

"Sorry," I smiled, "but you have to keep moving forward, finding better ways to do things. It's the future."

I pointed to the wood burning stove across the room. "Would you like me to start a fire in the stove? The storm is getting worse and it might be awhile before the power is back on."

"Do you know how? Billy always does that chore."

"Sure. Do you have any firewood?"

"Out on the back porch."

I walked over the uneven floors, through the kitchen, and into the enclosed back porch. This house was old, 1800s vintage. Emily would like it. She would see its character and want to restore it to its original stateliness. But me? I'd have it bulldozed and replaced with a new house and modern amenities. I preferred to live with today's technology if not tomorrow's. I'd love to have a room for a minicomputer, like the Data General Nova, and a plasma panel.

I loaded some wood into the stove and lit the fire. With the draftiness of this house, we'd need this fire if the power remained out for long, and it was doubtful that the power would be restored soon.

"Thank you, Robert. I'm glad you're here."

"Me too. I could have frozen to death." Those words just came out, but I didn't think about them until I heard myself say them. All I could think about was how long this storm would last, how I'd get my car dug out, how I'd get the files to the office, and, once I got them there, how we'd do the data entry faster. But there it was, I could have frozen to death. Even though I was safe, I didn't have things under control.

"Is your wife at home?"

"Yes. I hope she is OK." I realized then that I couldn't even call Emily.

"I've been praying that Billy is OK. I'll pray for Emily, too."

"Thanks," I replied. In our time together, I had learned that this was the best reply. Susie was always praying for someone or something. She was steeped in religion and her church, and that had been a frequent topic of our arguments.

Our last big argument was when she and her family were convinced that the world was about to end. She prosecuted her case every time we were together, claiming that the passing of a comet was a sign of impending doom. She would quote her evidence from the Bible. She would even leave notes in my locker with Bible quotes about the end times. I would tell her, *If the world is going to end, there's nothing we can do about it.* That infuriated her. She wanted me to go with her to a retreat for the event, but I told her I couldn't miss class. *I needed to get good grades in case the world didn't end*, I told her, but that only enraged her further. Needless to say, the world didn't end, but our relationship did.

It was not that I disfavored the church. It was that the church provided pat answers for all of the great questions about life, whereas I saw life itself as a journey toward those answers, a process of contemplation and questioning and discussion. But that was Susie, accepting and unquestioning, so it suited her fine.

"Do you have kids?" she asked.

"Not yet. Someday. Right now we're both focused on the business."

I knew that Emily was anxious to start a family, as anxious as I had been to start the business. She enjoyed programming and our business, but neither of us realized the intensity of the demand for our services. It was like a blizzard, like a whiteout. It obscured everything else, including children, a house in the country, a dog, and everything else that went along with family.

"It's vain to be a workaholic. Children are a gift from the Lord," she preached.

"Yeah, well, we need the means to raise them."

"The Lord provides."

"So you're still with the church even though the world is still spinning?"

"Yes, but not that church. It was too extreme."

You were pretty extreme, too, I wanted to say, but thought better of it. Maybe she had moderated a little. I wondered what I ever saw in Susie back then. She was pretty, and I suppose as a teenager that's all that mattered. The shape of her body, the color of her hair, the softness of her lips. She was popular, and socializing was her priority in high school. She never took the hard classes or seemed too concerned about her grades. She was content to get by and to embrace tradition rather than explore new things.

Emily and I, on the other hand, shared a what-if mindset about the world and a drive to learn and develop new technologies. To improve upon the past and build a better future. I was so lucky to have found her and to be married to her. Still, I wondered if we could endure, or whether we would lose control and find ourselves buried with snow in a ditch.

Evening came and still the blizzard blew against the aged house. Susie made soup and sandwiches, and we listened to the storm reports on her battery-powered radio. The radio said the storm was already one of the worst to hit northwest Ohio. Schools and businesses were closed. Roads, even the turnpike, were closed. They said it was the result of two converging weather systems, one from the north and one from the south. I worried about the data files in my car.

"So are your computers going to put me out of a job?" she asked.

"No," I replied. "but you might need to learn a little about computers."

"How am I supposed to do that?"

I walked to the telephone table and found a pencil and paper. I jotted down a few book titles. "Here are a couple of books I'd recommend. They cover computer basics for people who have never worked with computers before."

"Thanks, Robert," she said as she took the paper.

"You'll do fine. The more you know, the more valuable you'll be to the paper."

She nodded and sighed. "I guess I better get with the program."

I kept the wood-burning stove stoked, and the living room was comfortable. As night arrived, Susie brought out some blankets and pillows. She took the couch and I took the recliner. Some sleep would do me good. As I closed my eyes, I thought about Emily alone at home, probably worried about me, and I hoped that God would keep her safe and ease her worries. I also thought about Billy driving his snowplow, trying to maintain the roads against the fury of the blizzard. I hoped he would be safe, too.

The wind blew harder and louder at night. The old house creaked, and I had visions of it leaning like many of the old barns in Ohio farmland. I tried to put those visions out of my mind, but then another would appear, like a vision of the roof blowing off in the hurricane-like wind.

I dozed, only to fall into a troublesome dream. I was in the middle of a snow-covered field with Susie trying to light a fire to keep warm, but the north wind kept blowing out the fire. I wanted her to sit with me to block the wind, but she was praying and remained where she was. Then Emily came and sat next to me. We embraced. We kissed. I was able to light the kindling. Then the south wind joined the north wind and blew out the fire. I tried and tried to relight the fire. It was my one goal, my obsession. But the wind became a tornado. It scattered the embers. It lifted all of us above the grey, winter sky to where the sun shone. There were children, houses, dogs, data files, computers, cars, snowplows, footballs, doll flies, and toboggans all swirling in this single tornado, all shimmering in the sunlight.

When I awoke in the morning, I could hear the radio and Susie in the kitchen cooking. I looked out the window to see snow still falling, but the wind had subsided. There were 10-foot snowdrifts in the yard. I added some wood to the fire and walked into the kitchen. This ordeal would be over soon, and everything would be back to normal.

"The power and phone are still out," Susie reported.

"At least the wind let up," I replied.

The radio was reporting that the National Guard had brought in heavy equipment to help clear the roads. The drifts were too deep for regular snow removal equipment.

"I hope that Billy is at the maintenance yard," she said.

"I'm sure he is," I said, although I could not be sure of anything.

After breakfast I tried to find another radio station to see if we could get additional information, and I noticed that the radio had a VHF band that would receive police and fire frequencies. So I switched it to VHF and dialed around. I found the county sheriff's band, and that is where we heard the chilling police call. "All units, be advised that we have a missing snowplow and driver. Possibly in the West Creek area. The National Guard is clearing roads in that area now." A unit responded that he was near the area and would stand by.

Susie's face turned white. I wanted to say something reassuring, like the odds that Billy was the missing driver were low, or that if he got stuck he probably found shelter in a house like I did. I could not find the words, though. We sat by the radio for the rest of the morning waiting for further reports. I could picture the Guard's end-loader scooping snow from a road in the vast rural flatland and dumping it off the side of the road, a shovel full at a time, digging down to the level at which civilization lived.

At noon, I decided that I needed to do something productive. The snow had stopped falling, and there was a hint of sunshine. I put on my shoes and coat.

"Let me know if you hear anything. I'm going to shovel."

I grabbed the shovel next to the front door and began clearing the covered front porch, then the steps, then the sidewalk to the driveway. The snow depth was a few inches in some places, and more than ten feet in others. I had completed a path to the driveway when Susie called from the doorway.

"They said they found the snowplow," Susie explained as I entered. "The cop is on his way now."

I went in and sat next to Susie on the couch. We waited for the radio's silence to break. The deputy was probably driving down the cleared road to where the snowplow was found. The National Guard end loader was probably idling, the driver waiting in the road for the deputy.

The silence on the frequency was broken as the deputy identified himself. "The driver is in the truck," he said. Then, in struggled words, he continued, "He didn't make it."

"10-4," the dispatcher said. "We'll send transport."

Susie buried her face in her hands and sobbed. I put my arm around her and said, "We don't know if it's Billy." She nodded, pressing her tear-soaked face into my shoulder. Holding her felt so familiar, and the imperfections I had perceived about her seemed not to matter anymore.

"Please, Lord, don't let it be Billy," she prayed.

Yes, God, give us a break, I thought to myself.

I got up to check the phone.   If it was working, we could call the Maintenance Department, but there was still no dial tone.   There was nothing we could do but speculate about whether the deceased driver was Billy. Susie could sit in the house and pray, but I had to do something, so I went back outside to tackle the driveway. I carried the shovel to where the cleared sidewalk met the buried driveway.   It would be a challenging task, requiring focus and discipline.   I pierced the wet snow with the shovel and muscled out the first shovel-full. Then another and another, getting into to a determined rhythm.

I had only one goal that afternoon: clear the one lane driveway all the way to the road so that when the National Guard cleared the road, a car could drive up to the house.   Perhaps it would be Billy returning from work, returning to Susie and to the life they had planned. Perhaps it would be someone coming to tell Susie news she didn't want to hear.   Either way, there would be a clear driveway for the vehicle to enter and a clear sidewalk and porch for the person to walk.   It was a mundane goal, just maintenance, but it had to be done. There was peace in dedication to this simple goal.

Still, I could not focus on just this one goal. My mind wandered beyond the task at hand.   What if it was bad news? What if Susie's life would have to move forward without Billy?   What if Billy Jr. or Molly would never know their father?

What if it were me frozen dead in my car? Or Emily? There would be some business records and some money in the bank, but there would be no child. Who really had the grander goal, I wondered.

As I shoveled, I felt a new energy, a second wind. I was not frozen. I had survived, and within the blizzard's whiteout I had seen the whiteout that I had become. I knew what I must do.

By early evening, half of the driveway was clear. Down the road, I heard the powerful groans of an end-loader lifting snow and dumping it on the roadside. I could see its puffs of black smoke as it slowly made its way closer.

The driver could see that I wasn't done shoveling, so he waved me back and steered the end-loader into the driveway. In a few minutes, he cleared the remaining portion. I walked up to the side and signaled him. He shut off the engine and opened the cab window.

"Thanks for the help," I yelled. "Be careful, my car is in the ditch just up the road. On the right side."

"I'll watch for it.   Want me to lift it out with the shovel?" he joked.

"No, no, no! Just don't bury it further."

He let out a hearty laugh. "I'll watch for it."

The driveway was clear.   My task was complete.   I walked slowly toward the house, surveying the surrounding acreage.   The flat farmlands had been transformed into white rolling hills. Drifts covered every outbuilding and fence.   The unmerciful blizzard had sculpted such magnificent beauty. It had also destroyed and killed, knocking everything off balance. So it is with extremes.

I stomped the snow off my shoes on the porch. As I opened the door to go into the house, I saw a blue pickup truck turn into the driveway.

"Does Billy have a blue pickup?" I asked Susie.

"Yes," she replied.

"It looks like he's home."

She jumped to her feet and rushed out the door.

I watched as they embraced, then went to check the phone. The soothing sound of the dial tone was back, and I dialed our number.

"Hello?" Emily said hopefully.

"It's me," I said, and we were both in tears.

I told her about all that had happened, and she said she would come and pick me up. Then I said, "Emily, we need to buy a toboggan."

"Huh?"

"There's plenty of snow. We can take it to the big hill this weekend."

"Maybe," she said tentatively. "Do we have time for that?"

"Yes. And next year at this time, we can pull our baby around the yard on it."

The line was silent for a moment as I sensed Emily trending from stunned to ecstatic.

"Our baby?" she quavered. "Are you serious?"

"Yes. It's time. Maybe we can start on that tonight?"

Our Big Muley

Dad didn't need the house anymore. He had gone to be with Mom. As their only child, the task of preparing the house for sale fell to me, so I said good-bye to my wife and children and flew to Ohio from my home in California to do the work. It was an intense week of sorting through the artifacts of their 50 years in this house. It was exhausting physically and emotionally. Allocating only a week served to prioritize the physical work and keep the emotions in check. Emotions could be dealt with later.

A dumpster and a moving pod sat side-by-side in the driveway. A supply of moving boxes, packing tape, and bubble wrap sat on the floor of the living room when I began separating the keepers from the tossers.

Photo albums, letters, and certificates: obvious keepers and carefully boxed. They captured the images, thoughts, and accomplishments of their lives. They stored our family's times for future generations.

Boxes of canceled checks as far back as the 1960s: tossed in a garbage bag for shredding. They should have been tossed 30 years ago, but they had been saved just in case a question arose about whether a bill had been paid. Or in case someone wondered about the cost of a pair of house slippers in 1962.

National Geographic magazines from 1960 through the early 2000s: boxed for moving to my home. It was Dad's favorite magazine. The latest issue always sat on the toilet tank in the reading room, providing a window to the world and, now, a window to history.

Countless half-empty paint cans kept just in case touch ups were needed: tossed in a pile to be taken to the hazardous waste facility. Many of the interior and exterior colors had long since been painted over, but my parents grew up in the Great Depression. They threw nothing away.

Music boxes, ceramic figurines, and milk glass candy dishes: gently wrapped and boxed and labeled as fragile. Mom kept the house neat, orderly, and proudly adorned with these treasures.

A rusted Veg-O-Matic, a broken toaster, the chassis of a vacuum tube television set: relegated to the trash pile. They had been waiting in the basement workshop, hoping for repair by Dad, but they had out-lived availability of replacement parts.

So went the week of sorting, boxing, and tossing. Toward the end of the week, the physical work was done. The house, garage, and shed were empty. I made a pass through each to make sure I hadn't missed anything.

As I closed the shed door, I noticed an item I had missed. It was in the splash block outside the door. It had sat there since 1972 — 35 years — and perhaps that's why it went unnoticed. It had become part of the landscape of our family.

It was our Big Muley, and seeing it caught me off guard. I knelt down next to it. It looked exactly the same as it did 35 years ago, but it was different now. It was saturated with wisdom that I couldn't perceive back then.

It became ours in June of 1972. I had just completed my freshman year in high school. Mom, Dad, and I were preparing for our biggest vacation ever, a road trip out west. Dad was a millwright for the Folton glass company, which made windows for cars and plate glass for buildings. This was the first year he had three weeks of vacation, and years of planning had gone into this trip.

One goal was to see the west, including South Dakota and Wyoming. Another goal was to collect rocks, primarily agate, so that Dad could make bookends for the upstairs den. He had built bookcases in the den to hold our encyclopedias, books, and growing collection of *National Geographic* magazines, but he needed bookends to keep them orderly, erect, and in tight formation. Dad was not one to buy something he could make, and he could make just about anything given the raw materials.

We had taken shorter trips in previous years, including trips to the Great Smoky Mountains and Ontario, Canada. Those trips had given us experience with our equipment and our processes. We learned from each trip and applied that knowledge to the next. Those were our Mercury and Gemini days, but this trip out west was our Apollo program, our moonshot.

Our equipment was a military blue, 1968 Chrysler Newport with a V-8 engine and rear wheel skirts. Dad had installed a trailer hitch, heavy duty rear shocks, and a transmission cooler. Behind the Newport, we pulled an 18-foot Tow Low house trailer.

The Tow Low was a hard-roofed, telescoping trailer consisting of an inner shell and outer shell. For towing, the outer shell lowered over the inner shell so that the unit was about six feet high. At a campsite, the outer shell was raised by turning a crank in the front of the trailer, expanding it into a comfortable quarters with plenty of headroom. It had all the necessary amenities, including a propane stove, refrigerator, furnace, water tank, and two fold-down double beds.

When Dad got home from work at the glass factory, he and I would work on equipment preparations: changing the oil, lubricating the chassis, cleaning and adjusting the spark plugs, and checking the fluids. On the Tow Low, we would adjust the surge brake, lubricate the lifting cables, and touch up any paint on the chassis and propane tanks.

While Dad was at work, Mom and I would pack. Mom was a master at managing the household. She knew what was needed for cooking, cleaning, clothing, first aid, and other life necessities. From our previous trips, she learned how to scale that down to the limited space in the trailer and how to plan for resupply opportunities.

All of our preparation and packing activities were driven by checklists that I had typed on my manual typewriter. Those checklists had been refined after each trip, and by 1972 they were more complete than ever.

Our preparation was heavily influenced by TV broadcasts of space missions. They had imbibed us with a disciplined attitude, an attentiveness to details, an awareness of risks, and a practice of checks and cross-checks. The most recent mission, Apollo 16 in April, refreshed our mindsets just in time for this expedition.

On the night before we left, Dad backed the car into the driveway. We hitched the trailer and ran through the checklist for that procedure:
- Ball assembly secured
- Ball clamp locked
- Torsion bar clips secured
- Dolly pipe up
- Dolly wheel removed and stored
- Trailer brake off
- Safety chains secured
- Break-away chain secured
- Electric hookup connected
- Awning secured
- Crank locked

At 5:00 AM the next morning, the final countdown began, and we launched at sunrise.

Our first stop was the Naval Air Station in Ottumwa, Iowa. It was decommissioned by then and owned by the city, but when Dad explained that he had been stationed there in World War II, the security guard let us in to look around. The base was brand new when Dad arrived in 1943 to train to become a Baker, First Class. After completing his training, he shipped out to Pearl Harbor to run the Navy bakery there.

We drove through the base until Dad found the building where he had trained, then parked the rig and walked around. We peered into the windows as Dad peered into his memory.

"This is it," he declared. "This is the room where they trained the bakers."

He cupped his hands around the sides of his head and pressed his face close to the glass. "It looks like a storage room now. Is that a — ?" He choked up for a moment. "It is. There's a Hindger lathe in there!"

Dad had worked for Hindger both before and after his service in the Navy. It was his first real job apart from odd jobs at farms and restaurants to help the family survive the Depression. He had worked in the finishing department, filling and painting metal casings for their lathes and other machine tools.

"I probably painted that lathe," he said as he pulled away from the window.

Then he looked at the lower corner of the window glass, a habit he had acquired since joining Folton. He pointed at the insignia etched into the corner of the pane, a proud tear in his eye. "This is Folton glass!" he said.

Here in this place were artifacts of three periods of his life, of milestone experiences that had shaped him. The training room, the lathe, and the pane of glass were like museum pieces from eras of his life. They were gathered in this single spot and cried out *I was here* on his behalf. He shook his head in disbelief. What were the odds?

Hearing Dad's story as we exited the compound, the guard shook his head, too. "It's strange how things turn out," he said.

Our next stop was Mitchell, South Dakota. Dad's buddies at work insisted that we see the Corn Palace. After all, it was the world's only Corn Palace. It sat proudly on Main Street, its exterior decorated each fall with corn, grains, and grasses from the area. It was an event and entertainment venue and a testament to South Dakota agriculture. We stood across the street and marveled at the Mother-Goose-themed murals that adorned the outside of the building. Humpty Dumpty, the cow jumping over the moon, and the dish running away with the spoon were all illustrated using last fall's harvest.

We were three of thousands of tourists that year responding to the carney-call of this tourist attraction, who heard it holler *Come and see!* and *Spend money here!* Beneath the tourist din, though, were the heartbeats of artists thrusting the spirit of their lives upon this structure. Each fall they redesigned their magnum opus to the theme of the year, driven by that human passion for expression, that human need to create a permanence within the ever-changing landscape Tourists like us came to admire the artistry and appreciate the achievements of the area residents. Squirrels and birds came to feast.

Our next stop was Mt. Rushmore, where the faces of presidents Washington, Jefferson, Roosevelt, and Lincoln were preserved in the mountain. Nearby, we saw the work-in-progress on the Crazy Horse Memorial. The artists used their drills and dynamite to blast away the superfluous granite to expose the images of their visionaries, to immortalize the glorious stories of their peoples. No squirrels or birds would feast upon these objects.

Next we were welcomed to Yellowstone by bison, moose, elk, and bear. We set up camp at Fishing Bridge and spent days exploring the landscape, blistered like a teenager's pimpled face. We marveled at the reliability of Old Faithful, the steaminess of Castle Geyser, and the colors of the Fountain Paint Pots. We admired the terraces at Mammoth Hot Springs, where earth-heated water gently brushed minerals across the canvass of the landscape.

We learned about the magma in the mantle below. The heat and pressure within the heart of Earth choreographed the fluid performance on the surface. The Earth's passion drove the geysers to dance in the sulfured air, performing reliably and elegantly for its audience. The audience clapped and cheered and yelled *Bravo!* from the boardwalks.

Yet that same force was building pressure, lifting the crust, and tilting Yellowstone Lake. What of the day when this passion climaxes, when the magma pressure builds beyond what the crust can absorb? One day, the crust would give way and the magma would erupt, spewing ash and rock high into the sky and far across the globe. The sky would darken, and much life would suffer and die. The textured masterpiece painted on the crust would be ripped and scattered. Granite monuments would crumble to dust along with the stories they held. The Corn Palace would burn, and the fields would become unfruitful. That building in Ottumwa would collapse, scouring the paint from the lathe and shattering the window glass.

From Yellowstone we headed south, then east, stopping at Independence Rock in Wyoming. It was a dome of granite serving as a milestone along the Emigrant Trail during the western migration. Pioneers with their trains of conestoga wagons would try to reach this rock by Independence Day in order to avoid the mountain snowfall. When they arrived, they would have their names inscribed on it to say *I was here*. Just like the Corn Palace and Rushmore and Crazy Horse, it was a Hail Mary scream to the coming eons about their existence and endeavors.

Yet Yellowstone loomed, not to mention fires, floods, earthquakes, meteors, and maybe nuclear war. At 14 years old, that Hail Mary scream seemed to me a futile act. Nonetheless, I felt an itch to add my name to the rock as I explored the inscriptions around its base. I, too, wanted to say *I was here* to future generations. That would have been vandalism, of course, so I didn't.

We moved on to Fort Laramie to focus on the other goal of our trip, rockhounding. We pulled into a campground in town, and Dad skillfully backed the Tow

Low into its space. Once in position, we checked the level and determined how many leveling boards we needed under one wheel. Then we unhitched, and each of us went about our arrival tasks. Dad and I set the stabilizer jacks, cranked the outer shell up, connected the water and electric, and opened the outside awnings. Mom switched the refrigerator from gas to electric, then started preparations for dinner. Our tasks were second nature by now, and we all worked together as a team.

After dinner, we walked to the campground office to talk with the host about agate rockhounding sites. He was a Wyoming-weathered man with a cowboy hat and an earthy expertise about the area that he was eager to share. He grabbed a campground map, turned it over, and on the blank side drew a map to his recommended rockhounding site.

"When you get here," he said, "look for a gravel parking area where high voltage power lines cross the road. You'll see a trail. Take that to the fifth high voltage tower. That's the best place for agate. Now when you look for agate, you want to look for smooth nodules. Then look for a small indentation on the nodule and spit on it. Hold it up to the light and if it sparkles, you've got an agate. Remember, you have to spit on it."

With that map and training and a few paper grocery bags, we headed out the next morning to hunt for agate. We parked the car and hiked along the high power lines. We passed a small herd of cows grazing in the grass. They looked up as we passed, and I wondered what, if anything, they thought about us. They were content with their green grass and simple lives and had no passion for activities like rockhounding.   They had no need for bookends to prop up magazines that provided an understanding of the world.   They had no concept of history or lust for legacy. Nor did they have an awareness of hamburgers.

Large white clouds floated in the blue sky as we arrived at the fifth high voltage transmission tower. Along the trail and up a hill was a vast deposit of rocks. The campground host had given us good advice from a quantity perspective, and the three of us huddled to decide on a plan of attack. We decided that Mom would stay in the flatter areas so she didn't have to climb up the rocky hill. Dad and I would climb the hill then split up on the theory that fewer rock hounders would have picked over areas that were harder to reach. With our strategy decided, we each took a paper bag and headed to our search areas.

Near the top of the hill, I began my task of sorting rocks into keepers and tossers. I looked for a smooth nodule, then examined it for indentations. If there were no indentations, I tossed it back.   If there was an indentation, I spat on it and held it up to the sun. If it glistened, I placed it in my paper bag.

I had learned that agate was formed within hollows of volcanic rock. Water containing silica would fill these cavities, then the water would seep out or evaporate leaving silica gel deposits. Over millions of years, the deposits would build within the cavities until it was full. Within a nondescript nodule would be a beautiful agate with bands of translucent color. Spitting on the indentation provided a peek into what was inside.

I collected a dozen nodules, but they were all smaller than a fist, too small for bookends. I needed to find larger specimens, so I climbed to the peak of the hill. On the other side was a steep drop-off, but on the ridge I found a larger rock. It was mostly buried, so I used smaller rocks to dig around it.

As I dug, I couldn't help but to think about the Apollo 16 astronauts collecting rocks from Descartes Highlands on the moon. Astronaut Charlie Duke had climbed to the rim of Plum Crater to dig out a sample that had been spotted by team geologist Bill Muehlberger via the television camera. It was the largest rock ever retrieved from the moon at that time, and it was named Big Muley in honor of Muehlberger.

I continued to dig around my Big Muley, prying it from the grips of the earth where it had no doubt rested for millions of years. When I got it loose, I could see that it was the perfect size for bookends. It wasn't a smooth nodule and there were no indentations characteristic of agate, but it was big enough to be sawed into bookends that could hold erect a decade of *National Geographic* magazines. I spat all over the rock and held it up to the sun. If I turned it at just the right angle, I thought I could see a hint of sparkle, although it could have been just a sparkle of hope in my own eye.

I grabbed my bag and my Big Muley and made my way to Dad. "Look what I found," I said, handing it to him.

He took it into his hands. He turned it over. He spat on it. He held it up to the sun. I feared that he would toss it to the ground. I feared he would say, *Good try, but this is not agate,* but he looked at me and excitedly said, "I bet that is full of agate!" I was elated and reenergized, ready to continue the search for more potential bookends.

"It's going to be a job getting that back to the car, though," he pointed out.

"We can do it," I said. After all, the real Big Muley was too big to be stowed in their rock sample compartment, yet they found a way to get it back to Earth.

We continued to collect rocks as the white clouds darkened. We could hear thunder in the distance, so we decided to head back to the car with three partial bags of rocks and our Big Muley. It started to rain as we passed the cows, who continued to graze undeterred by the raindrops. They remained content; I felt the joy of accomplishment and hunger for a hamburger.

As it started to rain harder, we faced a problem. The paper bags were getting wet. The bag Mom was carrying fell apart and her rocks dropped to the ground. I added them to my bag, set the bag against my stomach, and pulled my shirt up to my neck to support the rocks and our Big Muley. It was slow-going as we slogged through the wet, but at last we reached the Chrysler and loaded our prizes into the trunk.

Like three Apollo astronauts, we drove back to the campsite, rendezvoused with the Tow Low, and set a course to our Ohio home. We unloaded the rocks and piled them in the splash block by the shed door.   In subsequent years, Dad used a diamond saw to slice the most promising agate samples, exposing their translucent rings of color, but our Big Muley sat untouched until that day in 2007.

When I noticed it in the splash block, I could see what I couldn't see back then.   I realized that Dad knew it contained no agate.   He knew it was just an ordinary rock, but he bet it was filled with something more precious than agate.   He bet it was filled with the memories of a Navy building, a Corn Palace, granite monuments, dancing geysers, mineral masterpieces, and names of pioneers inscribed on a rock.   He bet it was filled with the memories of the planning, teamwork, and drive that went in to our moonshot expedition.   Most importantly, he bet it was filled with the love in our family as we stood in the Wyoming landscape spitting on rocks. He was correct.

Some would think it silly, but I carried our Big Muley to the moving pod and packed it carefully with the other keepers. It would not last forever. If not destroyed by a Yellowstone eruption or some other disaster, it would someday pass to someone who knew nothing of the memories it contained and would be tossed away. That's the way of nature, but for now, I hold it dear. I enjoy the way it sparkles among my memories and the way it illuminates my own path through fatherhood.

Atop the Black Maple

Never married; no kids. That's the tag line that followed Roger through his 65 years on this planet. That's how he described himself when meeting new people. That's what he told the teller when opening a new bank account. Those were the boxes he checked on the form when having his will drafted. For better or worse, it would be the epitaph on his gravestone.

Roger sat on the bench along the river in his Ohio hometown. It had been a lifetime since he had been here. He had been to so many other places: Illinois, Rhode Island, North Carolina, California, Texas, Florida, South Korea, Japan, Hong Kong, Thailand, and Vietnam to name a few. Those places and experiences were the jigging lures that drew him though life like a bass. They kept him engaged, focused, and on the move. They kept him busy, at least busy enough to be content.

His hometown had grown, but this park and the river were much as they were when he was a boy. From the bench, he watched a dad helping his three young children fish from the dock. He watched him worm their hooks and cast their lines into the water. He watched him direct their attention to their red and white bobbers, no doubt instructing them to watch the bobbers closely to know when fish were biting.

Watching the dad made him think of his own father, who had often brought Roger and his siblings to this spot to fish. Roger's dad was a skilled fisherman and a great mentor who had given his children a tackle box full of wisdom, not just about fishing, but about life. Through those riverside talks, his dad had instilled optimism, confidence, and a sense of pride in Roger and his siblings, so much so that Roger hadn't even realized how poor their family was until after high school.

One of the kids on the dock squealed with delight while pulling a fish out of the river. The dad hurried to her side and helped her remove the small bass from the hook. She jumped up and down excitedly, then tentatively extended her hands as her dad handed the freed fish to her. Her face was aglow as she took the fish, giggling about its wiggling in her hands. Then her dad pointed to the river. The girl stepped forward, gently released the tiny fish into the water, and gave her a dad an enthusiastic hug as he lifted her up.

Never married; no kids. Roger wondered how it felt to be a father. To watch his own child glow with pride at catching a fish or playing a musical instrument or graduating from high school. To feel the hug of his own son or daughter. To have a progeny to whom he could pass his own tackle box of wisdom. But he turned off that path some 45 years ago right here along this river.

Roger reminded himself of all of the troubles along the path of marriage and children. The lack of freedom, the expenses, the arguments, and the compromises. The "never married; no kids" path had bypassed all of those pitfalls. It had spared him the wailing of babies, the chaos of over-active toddlers, and the persistent questions about things he didn't understand himself. It had spared him worries about their grades, about their illnesses and injuries, and about their encounters with bullies, boyfriends, and girlfriends. It had freed him from teaching them to read a book, solve a quadratic equation, throw a baseball, and drive a car. Over the years, Roger had built a hefty file of justifications for being "never married; no kids." Most of the time he believed them, but once in awhile, he wondered how he had let one setback change the course of his life.

The setting sun cast an orange glow over the river. Roger rose from the bench and ambled to his car. It was a brand new, ice blue, 1995 Mercury Gran Marquis LS. It was the most luxurious car Roger had ever owned, and it was a retirement gift he gave to himself. He breathed in the new car smell as he turned the ignition key. He pushed a tape into the cassette tape player, gently gripped the leather-covered steering wheel, and glided onto the road toward town.

He pulled onto Maple Street and into the driveway of his new home, a well-maintained house in the older part of town. He drove up the long driveway to the detached garage and eased his shiny vehicle inside. He opened the trunk and grabbed his suitcase, sleeping bag, and pillow. This would be his first night in his new home, and his furniture would not arrive until tomorrow. He'd have to sleep on the floor tonight.

By midnight, he realized that the wooden floor was too hard for his old bones, so he struggled to his feet and dragged the sleeping bag and pillow into the back yard. It was a warm, August night, and the grass beneath the towering black maple tree was comfortably soft. The fully leaved tree provided night-time shade from the brightness of the Sturgeon Moon.   The katydids and crickets sang their songs for him all night. *This was retirement paradise*, he thought to himself.

At sunrise, Roger opened his eyes to the unexpected shock of a young child standing in his back yard looking at him. He sat up and cleared the fog from his eyes. It was a boyish girl, about 10 years old with short black hair and wearing blue bib overalls.

She did not back away when Roger awoke. She stood her ground and asked, "Are you a bum?"

"No. I'm the new owner of this house. My name is Roger."

"My name is Juana. I live next door."

"Nice to meet you, Juana."

"My friend, Holly, used to live here. Do you have kids?"

"No, no kids."

"Did your wife kick you out of the house?"

"No. I'm not married."

"Are you divorced?"

"No. Never married; no kids."

"My dad left us when I was small. He didn't like me or my mom."

Roger didn't know how to respond to that, but mumbled, "I'm sorry."

"Me and Holly can climb this tree," she informed him.

Roger woke to the reality that this girl seemed to have no concept of boundaries, and there was no fence around his yard. Retirement paradise should have a fence around it. It wasn't just the intrusion of the girl onto his property that bothered him. It was that she brought a new worry for Roger, his liability should she climb and fall out of his tree. He added a fence to his mental to-do list.

"Well, I don't want you climbing my tree," he said bluntly.

"Juana!" her mother called from the house. Seeing Roger, she came out her back door and to the property line. "Juana, get back here. Breakfast is ready."

Roger rose and walked to the property line to introduce himself, explaining about the hard floors and that the movers would be arriving. Her name was Maria, and she told him she was a single mother and waitressing at the River Road Steakhouse downtown. She seemed friendly and respectful and doing her best to make a life for her daughter and herself.

Later that morning, the moving van arrived and parked in the street in front of the house. Down its ramp came all of his possessions. When he left this town at age

21 to join the Air Force, he had carried all of his possessions in a duffle bag. After a couple of decades in the military and a couple decades managing an apartment complex in Florida, a moving van and two young men were needed to transport it all.

Roger stationed himself inside to direct the placement of furniture and boxes. Roger had packed the boxes himself and had marked their contents so that getting everything into the correct room would go smoothly. This four-bedroom, one-and-a-half story, Cape Cod style house was the largest house Roger had ever owned, so there was more space than required for his belongings.

Juana followed the movers into the house and joined Roger in the living room where he was unboxing some wall hangings. She watched from behind him as he lifted a framed piece from the box and tore away the protective packing paper.

"You have a lot of stuff," Juana said.

Startled, Roger turned to see her. "What are you doing in my house?"

"The door was open."

"Well, you shouldn't let yourself in to someone else's house."

"I used to come here all of the time when Holly lived here."

"Well, she doesn't live here anymore."

"She moved to the other side of town where the rich people live," she explained. "Her dad got a better job. We probably won't be friends anymore."

Roger shook his head in confusion and leaned the framed picture against the box. He just wanted to get his retirement retreat set up. He didn't want a conversation with this girl. He didn't want interactions or worries or obligations. He was about to tell her to scram when the movers struggled into the room with a Hammond organ and asked where it should go.

"Down the hall to the right," he directed, then took a deep breath and looked at the girl.

"Juana, first of all, this side of town is no slum. It's a nice area with nice people. Secondly, you can still be friends with Holly even though she doesn't live next door."

"She'll probably join the Girl Scouts."

"You can join the Girl Scouts, too."

"No. It's for rich girls."

"That's not true. I grew up during the Depression, and my family was very poor. But I was in the Boy Scouts."

"Really?"

Roger picked up the framed picture. "This is a drawing of the house I grew up in. One of my sisters drew it. It's where all of those new houses are now, but back then, it wasn't in the town limits. It was an old farmhouse that we rented. It was in bad shape, but it was home for our six kids and my dad and mom."

Juana studied the picture. "Are you still poor?"

"No. I joined the Air Force, and after that I moved to Florida and managed an apartment complex. I saved money, and now I am retired."

"Why didn't you move near the rich people?"

"I could have, but I like this street and this house."

Juana considered that for a few minutes, then a broad smile lit up her face. It was a radiant smile, and Roger couldn't help but to smile back.

"I better go," she said, and she turned and left.

For a moment, Roger felt a vacuum in the room left by her exit, but his thoughts quickly returned to the task at hand when a mover carried a box into the room. "This one is marked high school books," he said.

"Down the hall to the left," Roger directed.

He was anxious to get his things moved in, unpacked, and organized. He was anxious to retreat into his retirement. The memories of his apartment management days were still fresh in his mind — showing apartments, doing the background checks, posting the rents, dunning the late payers, mediating disputes between tenants, and evicting the rule-breakers and deadbeats. The memories of his military days in personnel administration were there, too — recruiting and training airmen, developing policies and procedures, and notifying family members when an airman was lost. Those days, with all of their transactions, relationships, obligations, and disquieting challenges, were over. He would soon be able to curl up in his retirement cocoon and not worry about things like that, but he would need a fence.

Juana's daily visits grew increasingly annoying. She would appear in his yard whenever he was outside. Roger didn't want to be impolite, but sometimes he just had to be direct and terse with her. Other times he ignored her. Sometimes, like when he was waxing his car, he could do nothing to send her away. She sat cross-legged in the driveway the whole afternoon asking random questions and babbling about a range of topics.

By September, Roger had finished unpacking all of the boxes, hanging pictures, and feathering his retirement nest. Juana was back in school, starting fifth grade. That afforded Roger the freedom to be alone in the back yard on weekday mornings and afternoons. He could do yard work and watch the squirrels. Sometimes, he just laid under the black maple and watched the leaves beginning to change colors.

In the early evening, he retreated inside. He'd ensure that the doors were locked because sometimes Juana would come knocking on the door after school. Roger wouldn't answer the door, but he knew she would try to come in anyway.

One evening, Roger made himself a whiskey highball and sat in the recliner to reminisce through photo albums. The black-and-whites of his family taken in the 1930s and 1940s brought back happy memories. Despite the hard times, there were smiles on their faces and confidence in their eyes. It was as if their eyes were focused on something beyond their ramshackle, paint-bare house and their rag clothes and their empty pockets. Roger knew what those eyes saw; it was a shimmering light in the distance that his father had planted in their minds. Better days ahead. Better lives ahead.

Roger leafed through the album to 1950 and the pictures of his dad's car. It was a 1940 Oldsmobile Series

70 that his dad's late uncle had left to him. Roger had borrowed it many times for dates with his girlfriend, Evelyn. She was the shimmering light in Roger's eyes in those days.

Roger never really thought about their differences when they were dating. He saw her delicate face, her warm eyes, her perfectly-styled hair. He cherished her soft voice, her easy smile, and affectionate words. Of course, he had driven the Oldsmobile onto Evelyn's circular, blacktopped driveway to pick her up for dates. He had parked next to her dad's brand new, 1950 Cadillac. He had walked past the front yard statuary and onto the large, columned porch to knock on her door. Her dad had been quite successful financially, but Roger had been oblivious to that.

After high school, Roger got a job as a cook at a downtown diner, and Evelyn attended the local college. They continued to date, and they talked about marriage and children, at least until that day they strolled in the park by the river. That's the day she informed him that she couldn't marry him. Her parents did not approve, she told him. *You can do better* is what they told her.

There had been other opportunities: the waitress at the diner who always flirted with him, the girl who always sat next to him in the back pew at church, and Evelyn's friend who liked to walk with him along the river. In Roger's mind, none of them compared to Evelyn, so he turned onto the "married; no kids" path. It wasn't an immediate decision or even a conscious one. It was like being cut from the baseball team, then gradually coming to accept the idea that he didn't have what it takes to play the game.

He closed the photo album and consoled himself with the reasons "married; no kids" had been the better road. Maybe it was the whiskey, or maybe it was the newfound free time, but those reasons suddenly seemed insufficient. It was not that there was anything wrong with that path. Many chose it without regrets, but for Roger it left a vacuum. It left him holding a tackle box of wisdom with no sons or daughters to share it with. He poured himself another drink.

In October, the contractors began work on fencing the perimeter of his back yard. They dug the holes and concreted the redwood posts. Pallets of dog-eared cedar boards were stacked in the driveway waiting to be installed, and Roger was in the garage, organizing his fishing equipment.

"Would you like to buy some candy?" Juana asked. "It's a fund raiser for the school music program. I want to learn to play piano."

Roger was no longer startled at the sudden appearance of Juana. He had come to expect it. "No thanks," Roger responded. "I can't eat candy."

"You could buy some to give as a gift," she persisted.

"I said no," Roger replied.

Juana frowned and watched Roger hang his fishing poles on wall hooks he had installed.

"Are you going fishing?" she asked.

"No, just organizing the garage," he replied.

"I went fishing with my dad when I little," she said. "Then my dad left us. I've never been fishing since then. Mom doesn't like to fish."

Something in Roger nagged at him to take her fishing, to help her fulfill that desire, but he reminded himself that it was not his problem and that it would only encourage her further. He had other priorities. Soon the fence would be in place and he'd be able to enjoy privacy in his back yard.

With the arrival of November, the fence was complete. One Saturday morning, Roger put on his heavy coat, dragged a lawn chair under the black maple, and, without interruption, worked on his daily crossword puzzle. The last small batch of leaves rained down from the tree as he struggled with a crossword clue, "Walled off from the world." Ten letters. Starts with IRR. Ends with NT. His frustration with the puzzle began to grow.

Then a rake flew over the fence from Juana's house. Then a hand reached over the top. Then a leg. Juana pulled herself over the fence and landed on her feet in Roger's yard.

"Let's rake the leaves!" she called to Roger.

Roger's frustration with the puzzle fused with his frustration with privacy and threw Roger into an angry rage. He threw the puzzle and pencil into the air. He stood up and threw his chair across the yard.

"Dammit, Juana! I don't want you climbing over the fence. I don't want you in my yard!"

"But the leaves are down and it's time to rake," she responded calmly.

"Don't you understand? I want privacy. I don't want you coming over whenever you feel like it."

"I just wanted to rake leaves with you."

In an impassioned voice that frightened even Roger, he bellowed, "Go home! And don't climb over the fence again!"

Juana's face crumpled into a wretched frown. Tears showered from her eyes like the falling leaves. She walked to the fence as if she were going to climb back over to her side, but curled into a ball on the ground instead.

Roger was immediately remorseful about his stormy words. He never meant to hurt her feelings. He just wanted privacy. Was that so bad? Yet she persisted as if some force of nature was compelling her to engage him. Why couldn't nature just leave him alone so he could detach from the world like the leaves falling from the tree?

Roger walked to the fence and knelt down next to Juana. He put his hand on her back. In a gentler voice he said, "I'm sorry, Juana. I didn't mean to yell at you."

The curled ball sniffled and wiped her eyes.

"I'm sorry that I got angry. I know you just wanted to help rake leaves."

"I wish my dad was still here," she sobbed.

Roger looked up to the sky for whatever force of nature was putting him in this predicament. He wanted to say that he was too old for this, and that he was completely inexperienced and unqualified anyway. Roger had no idea how to respond to this girl, but these words came, "I can't do anything about your dad, but if you'd like, we can rake the leaves."

She stood up and put her arms around Roger's neck and hugged him. "I'm sorry for climbing over the fence."

He embraced her uncomfortably, then patted her on the back. "I'll get my rake and we'll get to work."

She pulled back, wiped her eyes, and her face blossomed into a huge smile. "Can I jump in the pile when we're done?"

"Sure."

They raked the leaves to the back of the lot, piling them on a rectangle of dirt where a garden had been. Roger could mulch them with the lawn mower later. They stood with their rakes, admiring the pile.

"Why do the leaves fall?" she asked.

"Well, all year, the leaves work to make food for the tree, but in the winter, the tree sleeps and doesn't need food. So the tree pushes the leaves off. Then it grows a new generation of leaves in the spring, and those leaves will feed the tree until the next winter."

Juana looked up into the black maple. "There's one leaf left near the top."

Roger looked, and sure enough, all of the leaves had fallen except for one. "The wind will probably blow that one off soon."

"Maybe the tree still needs that one," she speculated. "Maybe it hasn't finished its work yet."

"Maybe so," Roger agreed. "Are you going to jump in the pile?"

Juana smiled at Roger, dropped her rake, and leaped into the pile. Roger walked to the edge of the pile and heaped more leaves atop her. She giggled, and Roger remembered the giggle of the girl on the fishing dock in August, and he remembered the dad. It was a good feeling.

As she brushed the leaves from her overalls, Roger said, "Juana, how would you like to go fishing some time?"

"Tomorrow?" she asked.

Roger hesitated, then said, "Sure. If your mom says it's OK."

Her eyes and her smile were brighter than ever, and she gave Roger a hug.

The next morning, Roger backed the car out of the garage and put the fishing gear into the trunk. He brought both tackle boxes. The green metal one contained the line, lures, hooks, and bobbers. The other one contained the wisdom and stories that had accumulated over his lifetime, waiting for the chance to inform and inspire a younger soul.

Juana arrived, having walked in front of the house and up the driveway rather than over the fence.

"That leaf is still there," she pointed out.

Roger looked up to see the leaf that held tightly to its stem. It was brightly hued in yellow, orange, and red, with a black vein supporting each of its five lobes. The pointy ends were beginning to curl, but it was only slightly weathered.

"Yes it is," he acknowledged.

"Do you want me to climb the tree and bring it down?"

He opened the car door for Juana, and as he did, he caught a glimpse, just a momentary flash, of his own reflection in her eyes along with the glow of the morning sun behind him. It was brief. Like a sparkle on a lake, it was there one moment and then gone, but it was clear.

"No. I think the tree still needs it," Roger replied.

Old Vine Zin with an Old Time Friend

"I know it's been a long time since I've visited you," I say. "I'm sorry I've been away so long, but I've thought of you often over those years. When I heard the news, I knew I had to see you again, one last time."

Now I don't normally talk to inanimate objects, but it seems acceptable given the circumstances. Besides, there's no one else around. It's just me and the bridge and a couple bottles of wine on this Sunday evening. Day hikers have gone home to their dinners and showers and preparations for their workweeks. Fishermen have reeled in their lines, closed their tackle boxes, and left with their stringers of fish. Kayakers have passed under the crumbling arches of the bridge for the last time. Tomorrow will bring diesels, dynamite, and demise.

I look up at you from the riverbank and tremble with discomfort. You are more frail and decrepit than I expected. That solid, graceful shape that I remember is gone, and your body is covered in scars. I look away, not wanting to embarrass you as you lay naked under the clear July sky.

"I hope you remember me," I say. "I hope you remember those happy times we had, you and me and my friends. The first time you saw me I was a little boy, maybe three years old. I remember it from a photo. I was with my dad over there on the riverbank. I had a string on a stick. My dad had clipped a red and white bobber to the string and had put a worm on the hook. I'm a grandfather now."

Of course, that bridge has seen more years than I would ever see. Built in the early 1900s, it's more than a century old now. When it was built, it was the longest bridge of its type in the world. Its twelve graceful arches supported the rail bed for an electric railway that carried passengers and goods between major cities.

I sit on the riverbank with my back against the wall of the first arch. When I was a boy, my friends and I searched for Native American arrowheads here. We pawed through the rubble looking for flat limestone that had been shaped and sharpened by ancient tribesmen. We'd always find a few. Now I paw through my backpack looking for my corkscrew. Finding it, I cut the foil on the bottle and remove the cork, then pour a glass of my favorite Old Vine Zinfandel.

"Here's to old men and old bridges," I toast as I touch the glass against the weathered concrete of the bridge. With my finger, I flick some of the wine onto the concrete for my old friend to enjoy. "After decades of weekend wine tasting in California, this is my favorite. You probably can't get this here in Ohio, so I brought a couple bottles to share with you."

I breathe in the comforting bouquet of the Zin and sip its soothing smoothness. It will relieve some of the discomfort of this visit as well as other lingering pain.

"Do you remember," I inquire, "when I was in the Boy Scouts and we had a campout just upstream? One boy stole a can of Right Guard from another boy and we tossed it around, playing keep-away with it. Then someone threw the aerosol can into the campfire. The scout leader hollered at us to get away from the fire. We all backed away as the can exploded and launched upward in a misty ball of flame, then fell into the river and was swept away. The scout leader gathered us for a stern lecture about campfire safety. You were there in the background during our scolding. You were in good shape then."

I sip wine as I remember that image. The square-chinned scout leader spewing impassioned words about fire safety as he beat the Boy Scout Handbook against his hand. And behind him, the immotile bridge, strong and solid, providing backbone to his every word. The bridge was a masterpiece of engineering, a product of discipline and hard work, and a symbol for every word the scout leader spoke.

"Your picture was everywhere back then," I say. "On the village limit signs, on the Town Hall, on police cars and fire trucks, on newsletters and stationery. They adopted you as the village symbol."

I splash the last remaining swig of my wine onto the concrete, then pour another glass. Who knows whether red wine stains concrete? It doesn't matter now. These days bring freedom from concerns like that.

"Do you remember Beth?" I ask. I look up at the skeleton of the bridge and wait for an answer. My lips tremble and a lump forms in my throat. I swallow it along with a gulp of wine. I look away from the bridge and focus my eyes on the area where I sit, remembering. "We would come here when we were in high school. We'd sit right here beneath this arch listening to the sound of the river washing over the limestone riverbed."

I can almost see her sitting next to me now. The first time we came here was for lunch one Sunday. We both worked weekends at River Road Market just a couple of blocks from here. She was a cashier and I was a stock boy. I got up the nerve to ask her to lunch, and we ended up brown-bagging it here under the bridge.

"The first time we came here we talked for a couple of hours," I say. "We were late returning from our lunch break and got in trouble. You could have reminded us about the time, but you didn't. And I thank you for that."

I tap my glass against the concrete in thanks, take another sip, and continue. "You were a good friend to me. Trustworthy. Like the time I snuck a can of beer from the cooler at the store. Beth and I sat right here and shared it. It was the first time we tried beer and neither of us liked it, but then we had our first kiss here, and we both liked that."

I remember the wetness of her lips and the softness of her face as I touched her cheek with my hand. Her innocent and longing blue eyes. Her radiant blonde hair. Most of all, I remember that feeling of connectivity between us. I felt it at that moment, after that kiss, and I still feel it today.

"What about that thunderstorm? Do you remember that time?" I ask as I finish my glass of wine and pour another. "The rain came down by the bucket. No space between the drops. Beth and I sat here under your arch, and you gave us shelter and kept us dry. We huddled together and kept each other warm. The lightning struck close, but you protected us."

Beth loved music, and she was learning the guitar. She didn't like me to listen while she was practicing, but once she was comfortable with a song, she would play it for me. We'd sit here and she'd play. She had an angelic voice.

I sit silently for awhile, just listening, wishing I could once again hear her sing. The sun is setting now, yet the evening seems so empty without Beth's voice. The birds are melodious, but it's not the same. I pour another glass of wine and flick some onto the concrete for my friend.

I think back to high school graduation. The night of graduation, after the ceremony and backyard parties, Beth and I and a group of our friends came here under this first arch. We started a bonfire and sat around it, our faces reflecting the orange flame and the newly found freedom in our lives. Our required education was complete, and our future was ours to decide. There were no more school buses to catch, no more class schedules, no homework due. It was a terrifying freedom, not unlike the terrifying freedom I feel now. It was forcing us all to look forward and make big decisions, but at least for that one night, we looked backward. Celebrated. Partied.

"Do you remember that party?" I ask. "You were such a gracious host to put up with our raucous gathering. It was loud, especially the fireworks that someone launched over the river. There was alcohol. Some had weed. Later in the evening, it calmed down as the rowdy ones left. Then it was Beth and me and two other high school couples. The fire died down to embers and Beth brought out her guitar."

It is growing dark now. Even the birds are silent, and I long so much to hear Beth sing like she did that night. To hear the soothing sounds as her fingers caress her old guitar. The song was "We May Never Pass This Way Again" by Seals and Crofts, a song well-suited for a high school graduation. After a couple more swallows of wine, I hum the tune. It's ingrained in my soul, as are the lyrics. I sing it as I think about the fullness of my life, as I take comfort that I heeded the words of that song. My dreams did not slip away, and I found the courage to sail life's sea. Beth and I found the courage together.

"You know this," I say, "but after the other couples left, I asked Beth to sing that song again. And when she was done, after she sang that part about not passing this way again and wanting a life with you, I asked her to marry me. You know how happy I was when she said yes."

I choke up thinking about that night. I refill my wine glass. There's a little left in the bottle so I give that to my friend. If I were still a teenager, I'd throw the empty bottle against the concrete to see and hear it shatter into tiny pieces. That youthful fascination with destruction has long since disappeared, replaced by an acute awareness of the fragility of everything. I put the empty bottle into my backpack.

"Another thing about that night," I continue. "Beth and I were cuddled together looking across the river. I remember seeing the yellow glow of lights in the tall building beyond the tree line. It was the dormitory of the university. Both Beth and I would attend starting in the fall. It was comforting, like a shimmering light beckoning to us, showing us the way."

Our plan was to complete our four years of college and then marry after we graduated. I thought I wanted to be a civil engineer so I could design bridges and roads. My interest changed after my first year of college. The thing about a shimmering light beckoning to you is that the shimmering light, well, shimmers. It moves, so you have to pursue it. After my first year, I found myself more inspired by the computers I was using than the engineering problems I was solving with them. So I changed my major to computer science. Beth's dream was music, and she never wavered from that. It was in her DNA.

We still came to the bridge during our college years. We'd come in the late spring after the ice flows cleared. And we'd come in the summer and fall. Fall was most beautiful with the oranges and reds all around us and the calmer river current.

"You know that fall, just before we started college?" I say. "That's when I first noticed something wrong. Beth and I were sitting here and we kept hearing little splashes in the river. I thought it was fish jumping, but it turned out to be little chunks of your concrete falling into the water."

As I sip my wine in the darkening night, I listen for those splashes and for that other noise, that sound of dirt and stone leaking from the bridge's broken carcass and pouring into the river. All I can hear is the rushing river as it drowns out the erosion of my friend's existence.

"I don't know if you know this," I say, "but one year there was an effort to help you. There was a committee trying to convince the state to repair and preserve you. Some wanted to give you a bicycle trail and walking trail. Some wanted to make you into a garden. Beth and I volunteered to get signatures on a petition. We walked the neighborhoods and stood outside stores and shops. I want you to know that no one refused to sign. Everyone we spoke to supported the petition. You were dearly loved."

I sip my wine and smile, thinking about those days as hope turned into confidence. All of those signatures, all of those hearts buttressing our cause. How could anyone deny our request? But they did. They said the bridge served no transportation purpose, so they could not justify spending transportation dollars to restore it. My heart was broken even though I understood. And today, as I sit here with my wine and an expiring timespan, I am consoled and thankful to have known the bridge.

I continue, "We were there that day when two of your spandrels collapsed. I'm sorry that I couldn't help you."

It was a spring day and the river was loud, but the sound of the collapse was so much louder. An entire arch out over the river failed. The concrete cracked and large chunks fell into the water. The dirt and stone within the arch spewed like blood and guts from the open wound. It was the beginning of the end.

It seemed like everything started falling apart after that, starting with the closure of the River Road Market. When Beth and I arrived for work one Sunday, the owner called us into his office. He said he had been trying to sell the business, but no one would buy it. A chain grocery store had moved into town, and no mom-and-pop store could compete with their prices. So we were out of our part-time jobs.

"Then Beth's dad got sick," I say. "He was a welder at a factory. He had been an active man and strong, like you. He coached Beth's softball team when she was a girl. Then he started having trouble breathing and chest pains and coughing. They diagnosed him with mesothelioma. Beth was so distraught. Then other factories started closing down and moving south, and people were losing jobs. It seemed like everything was collapsing in those days."

I finish most of my glass of wine and give the rest to the bridge. I feel lightheaded, like my head is spinning, and I long to put my arm around Beth, pull her close, and cuddle like we always did. Instead, I press my back firmly against the wall of the first arch. It's hard to cuddle with a bridge, but I need to feel its presence. It's the last night we'll be together, and we will never pass this way again.

"Do you remember our wedding?" I ask. "It was right here under this arch. Right here where I had proposed. It was difficult for Beth's dad because he was in such bad shape, but he walked her down the aisle. We said our vows right here in front of our family and friends and you. To love and to cherish till …"

I take a sip of wine, and then another. I reach into my backpack and pull out my wallet. I remove a photo and hold it up for the bridge to see.

"This is Beth in her wedding dress that day." I say. "She was more beautiful than ever. Really, though, she grew more beautiful with each anniversary we celebrated. I wish you could have come with us to California. I wish you could have been part of our lives after our wedding."

We moved to Silicon Valley after graduation so I could take a programming job with a computer company. Those were exciting times with constant waves of new technology. We'd build something new and better, then begin another project to make it even better. It just lifted me up and up and up. And Beth was immersed in music, teaching music and writing songs and performing in a band.

"We raised two children," I explain. "They would have loved to come here to the river and see you. And our grandchildren would have loved to come here, too. Those kids and grandkids became the most important parts of our lives, even more important than computers and music.”

I pull out more photos and hold them up for the bridge to see. They are our children and our grandchildren. Then I put them all back in their places in my billfold and return the billfold to my backpack. With a sigh and a tear, I look up to the bridge and tell it the news, “Beth passed away last year.”

I can’t say more because the lump in my throat formed again. I fight back tears, not wanting to cry in front of my friend. I rest my elbows on my knees and cover my face. I didn’t intend this visit to be about my sorrows. I just wanted to pay a visit before the demolition crews arrived, but everything is so intertwined.

“I’m sorry for your loss,” comes a deep voice, echoing under the arch.

“Thank you. I — ” I look up and all around to find the source of the voice. Could someone have come by in the dark of the night and listened to my laments?

“Hello?” I ask.

“Beth was a wonderful person. I know you miss her,” comes the voice again.

“Who is there?” I ask.

“It’s me, your old friend.” His baritone voice is slow and resonate.

I stand and look around in the darkness, still not believing my ears. Then I stumble to my backpack for that second bottle of Zin, uncork it, and pour a glass. “I think I need another drink. Would you like some?”

"Sure, just a little," he replies. I splash some from the bottle onto the wall of the arch.

"Thank you," he says. "I'm not much of a wine connoisseur. Everything tastes like water to me, but I appreciate your thoughtfulness."

"I didn't know you could talk," I say.

"I don't normally talk to animate objects, but it seems acceptable at this point," he replies. "I'm glad you came to see me."

"Do you know what is happening tomorrow?" I ask.

"Yes, I do," he replies stoically. "Workers in hard hats came around making their plans."

"I'm sorry. I wish it wasn't going to happen."

"It's OK," he replies. "I appreciate your past efforts to restore me, but it's time."

"So you remember me?"

"Of course. I remember everything, including a few things you didn't mention earlier."

"Like what?" I inquire with a little trepidation.

"Oh, like who threw the can of Right Guard into the campfire."

"Oh that. I don't know why I did that. I just got caught up in the game."

"And other things, like the other girl."

A wave of guilt passes through my body, a guilt that I long ago packed away into a box and buried in the backyard of my conscience. I took a few mouthfuls of wine as if that would help. "Cindy. Yes, I brought her here not long after I brought Beth. She was a popular girl. Pretty."

"A good kisser, it seemed."

"Yes, that. I don't know why I brought her here."

"You wanted to get into her pants."

"I guess," I say shamefully, trying again to wash away the guilt with wine.

"It's OK. If I were a teenage boy I'd want to get into her pants, too."

I look up at the bridge, comforted by his apparent forgiveness. "Right from the start, there was always something special about Beth. I realized that after my date with Cindy."

"Dates," he corrected.

"OK, yes, dates," I admit, "but it didn't take long for me to realize my mistake and how special Beth was. She was a sparkling light. I felt that connection right away, but I didn't immediately realize how significant that was."

"I understand. It takes dark to show light. At least that's what I gather from the artists who used to paint portraits of me."

"I remember those artists," I say. "They would set up over there in the grass with their oils and brushes and paint you. Sometimes they'd have classes where whole groups would come to paint you. I have a print of you from one of the artists."

"It was flattering," he says. "My youthfulness and usefulness were gone by then, so there was consolation in posing for artists."

"I didn't know you before then."

"When I started out, I was part of the railroad era, carrying the electric railroad across the river. About the time I got here, the old canal system was being closed down. It was exciting to be part of the new era, but it was sad to see the demise of the canal era."

I pour another glass of wine and give some to my friend. "I used to walk on the old towpath trail right over there," I offer.

"Yes, that was closed down when I was built. Floods finished off the canal system. Back then, I was so confident and optimistic. I thought I was part of something that would last forever. I thought I was pretty special."

"Well, you were. You were the longest bridge of your type in the world," I remind him.

"Yes, but things change. About 30 years later, the electric railway closed down. Trucks and cars replaced it. I wasn't so special after all. Hey, how about another splash of wine?"

"Sure." I splash a little wine from my cup and take a drink myself.

"There was a time when they put me back to work. The steel bridge downstream collapsed, and there was a steel shortage because of World War II. So they put a roadbed on me and I carried one lane of cars and trucks back and forth over the river. The cars and trucks were not as gentle and graceful as the electric railway. They were loud and smoky and rough on my roadbed, but it was fun to be doing something useful again. When that ended, the artists brought some comfort to me. Now I just savor my remaining days and reminisce about the old times."

"I wish I could have helped you. I tried."

"Yes, you did. I am thankful for your efforts. It's nice to know that so many people supported those efforts, but I also understand the final decision. Eras come and go. People and things come and go. You find your purpose, fill it the best you can, and make friends along the way. That's all you can do."

I think about that night long ago, sitting here and seeing the lights of the university dormitory above the tree line on the other side of the river. I look now and see darkness there. The trees have grown and block my view as if to say there is no longer a viable path for me there.

"I found my purpose at the university," I say. "It took me to Silicon Valley to work on computers. It was a good run. Fulfilling. I'm retired from that now. Like you, I savor the days and reminisce, but is that all there is to it?"

"I wish I knew. Everyone does. I've listened to people sitting there on the riverbank talking about it, some with theories of what it's all about, some with poetry that yearns for answers. All I can do is look up into the star-soaked night sky, wonder at its enormity, and accept my smallness. I'm just a bridge, and have to trust that there's far more than I can understand."

I stand, then walk out from under the arch. I look up at the night sky. It's a moonless night. The sky shimmers with billions of stars. I, too, feel the smallness. I know I will feel the emptiness when my friend is gone. More than anything right now, I feel the loneliness without Beth. I finish my glass of wine, sit under the arch, and pour another.

"I miss Beth so much."

"I know you do," he consoles. "I know how I would feel if this river dried up. It's been my partner for so long. I wouldn't be who I am without the river."

"It's not like I have a lot of years left myself. But how do I go on without her?"

"Well, I'm not an expert," he begins, "but I imagine you do what you've always done. You look for a light, a light that shimmers to attract you. You'll know it when you see it, but you have to search for it. When you see it, pursue it to wherever it takes you."

I hear a pop from across the river and walk out from under the arch to see what it is. I stand on the edge of the shoreline, the waters flowing by in front of my toes. I hear another pop, and a bottle rocket launches into the sky across the river. It's a single flare rising upward along its given trajectory, then blossoming into a hundred petals of color, reaching out in all directions. Then all of the embers go dark and unseen as they continue their journey downward, touch the water, and are carried away by the river.

I return to the arch and lie down beside its concrete wall. "Fireworks," I tell the bridge. I grow sleepy and close my eyes. "Probably teenagers with leftover fireworks," I say to the bridge, but I hear no response.

"Good night, old friend," I mumble as I drift off to sleep. "Good night, old Zin," I add as I relax my grip on the wine glass.

I awaken in the early morning to the sound of diesel trucks. I hear a woman's voice hollering to someone in the distance. "Hey, boss," she yells, "there's somebody sleeping here."

I open my eyes as she shakes my shoulder and bends down to me. She's wearing a yellow hardhat and an orange construction vest. "Sir, are you OK? Wake up, sir."

I sit up as an orange-vested man, also in a hardhat, joins her. "Hey buddy," he says. "What's going on here? How are you doing?"

My head hurts as I struggle to my feet. The man and woman help steady me as I rise.

"Are you a protester?" the man asks.

"What? No," I reply.

"It's OK if you are," he continues. "No one on the crew wants to see this happen either. We're all hoping for a last-minute stop-work order."

"I was just here to see my old friend," I say.

"For your safety," the woman explains, "we need you to move up to the parking lot. Do you need a place to go? We can take to you to the shelter to get cleaned up and have something to eat."

Realizing what they must think, I gather my things. "No, I'm fine. My rental car is in the parking lot. I'm staying at a hotel near the airport."

I pull myself together and walk to the parking lot. As I head toward my rental car, I see heavy construction equipment being unloaded from flatbed trucks. There are dump trucks and end loaders and a huge crane.

I see a group of orange-vested workers, and I give them a wave as I pass by. I get in my car. Pulling out of the parking lot, I see a crowd people carrying *Save Our Bridge* signs at the parking lot entrance. I give them a wave and a thumbs-up as well.

I rub my mourning eyes, pull onto the highway, and head east into the shimmering light of the rising sun.

About the Author

Rich Thayer was born and raised in northwest Ohio. In high school, he developed a passion for writing, and in college, a passion for computers. After earning a computer science degree, he combined those interests in a 32-year career in technical communication. He moved to San Jose, California and worked as a technical writer and technical publications manager for several Silicon Valley technology companies. Retired from technical writing, he now writes fiction. *Into the Shimmering Light* is his debut short story collection. Rich and his wife, Glenda, reside in northern California.